sexy tales of paleontology

PATRICK LENTON

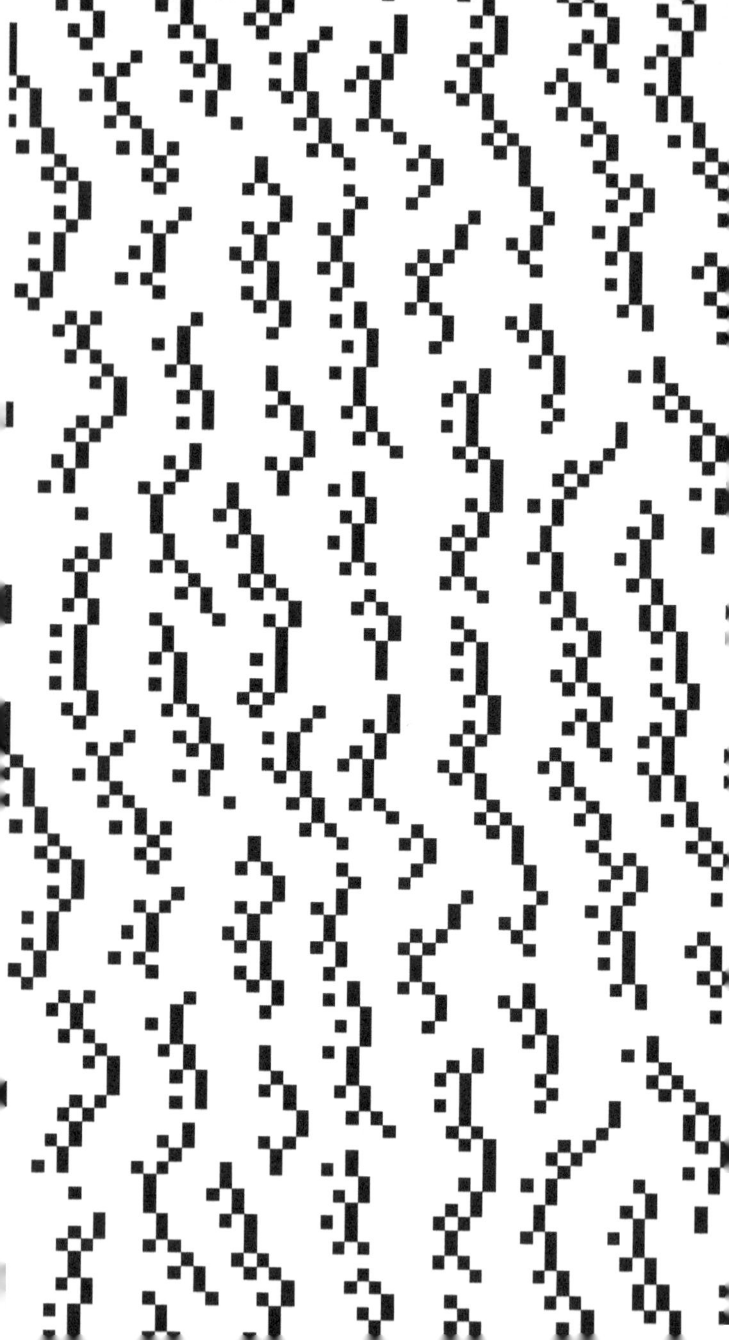

First published 2021
by Subbed In
www.subbed.in

Book and cover design by Dan Hogan
Text set in 8pt Domaine Text

First edition

Printed and bound in Birraranga (Melbourne)

National Library of Australia Cataloguing-in-Publication:
Lenton, Patrick
Sexy Tales of Paleontology / Patrick Lenton
ISBN: 978-0-6451524-4-9 (paperback)
ISBN: 978-0-6451524-7-0 (eBook)

Subbed In 014

These stories were written and edited on the stolen land and waterways of the Gadigal-Wangal people of the Eora nation. This book was printed and bound on the stolen lands of the Woiwurrung (Wurundjeri) and Boon Wurrung people of the Kulin nation. Sovereignty was never ceded. Patrick Lenton and Subbed In pay their respects to elders, past and present.

Always was, always will be Aboriginal land.

Contents

6   43 rats

18   The Doctors Murphy

36   The man who shot the moon

54   That's chess, baby

68   Home is where the dad is

76   A letter from a dying soldier to his sweetheart who he had never fulfilled sexually

80   Beach bodies

84   Control variable

94   Untold tales of kindness and charity

104   The Dog Park

112   Egg

116   Farewell, Stars Hollow

126   Jim Kardashian

142   Homing pigeon

144   The Anniversary

154   Jimmy and the Killbot

166   The good boy below

176   The Little Crane

184   Together

192   Sexy tales of paleontology

200   Boatjack I

226   Boatjack II

244   Boatjack III

43
RATS

By my 28th year, my trenchcoat had become a ragged thing.

It still did the job — it wrapped tightly around me, cinched off with a long belt like a hangman's noose, buttoned from top to bottom. It was a dark grey like a sad winter's afternoon, and it had flaring lapels as dramatic as a startled pigeon taking flight.

It was functional, this trenchcoat of mine, but it was showing its age. It was threadbare in places, and once a hole appeared it seemed almost impossible to patch it up. People could see through it, much to my dismay. The trenchcoat had one goal after all, and that was to cover.

And I think it was because the trenchcoat was becoming less structurally sound, that people started to notice it more. When I walked down the street, I noticed that people who would normally ignore me, began to cast their eyes over me, with a menacing sideways eyelid blink.

Broad men at gas stations who would usually just see a nice sensible trenchcoat, would flick their tongues out and taste something on the air when I walked by, and they'd rub their ham-fists together threateningly, or nudge their compatriots, and turn their long necks to watch me walk past.

Once I was followed down an alleyway by a man who hissed slurs, until I ducked into a jazz bar, forcing me to enjoy some smooth saxophone improvisation until I was sure he'd slithered past.

Or, like once when I was at a work Christmas party and was drawn into a loud heated conversation with several of my colleagues, who flapped and squawked around the table, cigarettes held akimbo, glasses of sauvignon blanc splashed with gaudy abandon, and instead of treating me with the casual professional disinterest I'd enjoyed for the last four years, they began poking the trenchcoat, trying to find out what was under it. I knew they meant no harm precisely, but I fled, with their laughter and raucous cries swooping, encircling me.

When you're 43 rats crammed into a trenchcoat, you don't particularly want people to question what's underneath.

My best friend Clare came over to my house, so we
could drink wine and say terrible things about the
people we called our friends. We were very similar
people, Clare and I — pretty motivated, disciplined,
kept to ourselves, and loved to watch shows about
devastating British murders on a long cold beach or in
a quaint yet cursed rural village. She was also, notably,
an angry ginger cat in a huge fancy hat.

For as long as I'd known Clare, people had commented
on the hat, an enormous Carmen Miranda style affair,
covered in fruit and flowers and surrounded by an
enormous brim. It eclipsed her face like a UFO on the
horizon of a long rural highway. People would look at
the hat first, never noticing that an absolutely furious
ginger cat sat underneath it. I guess people never
particularly think that a cat might be sitting amongst
them, especially when there's just such a huge hat
to talk about. However, even though we were good
friends, we never talked about the fact we were animals
covered in clothes. We just never did.

That night as we sipped cheap wine and Clare
stretched luxuriously and coughed furballs
comfortably, I mentioned that my sweet, nervous
mother had taken me aside recently.

'Darling,' she'd asked, immaculately manicured nails
absently caressing her long string of pearls. 'Are you …
are you sure you're happy in the trenchcoat?'

I always laughed if people brought up the trenchcoat,
and I did it again. 'Sure,' I said, 'you know me!'

But, in an out of character move for that extremely
repressed woman, she looked me in some of my many
eyes, and placed a hand on my coat's shoulder pads,
and said, 'you deserve to be happy.'

I laughed again.

Clare got mad when I told her this, striding furiously
around the room.

'Oh my god, people need to mind their own business, if
you want to wear a trenchcoat, you're allowed to wear
a trenchcoat, maybe the trenchcoat is who you are,
maybe there's nothing wrong with a trenchcoat? What
the actual fuck, I can't believe I just said trenchcoat so
much!'

What Clare was saying was pretty much what I'd
always thought, but at that moment, in that room, the
trenchcoat felt like a straitjacket.

'Yeah,' I chuckled, 'it's kinda like your hat.'

'I actually don't know what you're talking about,'
answered Clare.

Not long after that, a friend of mine asked me to come
out to a bar I knew was almost exclusively fraternised
by woodland creatures — voles, otters, badgers,
bears, twinks, weasels, libertarians, deer, etc. I'd never
particularly found these kinds of places welcoming.
If most places tended to see the trenchcoat as a
disguise, and ignore my seething body of vermin, then

these kinds of people viewed the trenchcoat as a real insult. They wanted to live in a world where woodland creatures didn't have to wear human clothes, which I thought was great and really brave and cool and all, but I didn't really see what it had to do with me.

Perhaps it was the endless shots of Jägermeister, perhaps it was the knowledge that no snakes were allowed in this bar, with their hooded gaze and their rattling tails, but I danced in ways that I'd never danced before, because dancing was a very quick way of showing that underneath my trenchcoat writhed 43 rodents. My friend Stephen just smiled when I loosened the belt of my coat and undid a few buttons in the steamy heat. I felt wild and reckless, and I allowed a devil-eyed hare to caress me near the strobe lights. But when I felt his hands near the next button, I woozily pushed him away and fled out into the refreshing cold air of the street. Stephen didn't invite me again, and the trenchcoat picked up a stain, like booze, or maybe blood.

I met a nice girl at the improv comedy class I did, which was recommended to me as a way to 'come out of my shell' a little more. I don't know how much it helped me change in my day-to-day life, but it certainly served as a good introduction for Jess and me. If you can still find someone attractive after watching them do improv, then you might as well get married immediately. Jess was funny and weird, and even though I worried about her reaction when she peeked under the trenchcoat, there was something about her that made me think it might be alright if she did.

One of the things I liked most about Jess was her passion. She truly believed people could work to change the world. I wasn't sure myself. I only needed to look at myself, wrapped in the same trenchcoat for my entire life, to know that transformation was more difficult. Still, it was nice to feel hopeful.

Around the same time as I was seeing Jess, I discovered that Clare was seeing somebody. She became harder to pin down, evasive, non-communicative. When we'd finally catch up for coffee, it had the energy of a chore, an obligation. I didn't know why, until one day I saw her walking down the street with the girl she was clearly seeing. She seemed more vibrant, happier. I also noticed that she'd matched hats with the girl, sporting a cool new baseball cap. It suited her, a cool urban cat. When I looked on her social media, she only seemed to be in photos with people wearing the same caps. Sometimes they were other cats, mostly not. But always the caps.

I had a run in with a snake again, this time walking home from work in the soft evening gloom, lost in a podcast. All I had for warning was the sudden startling sight of a long-scaled face in front of me, and then fists. I couldn't hear the hissed things said, due to the podcast about murders playing ominously in my ears, but I could feel the venom long after. I wasn't hurt too bad, but it's hard to be 43 rats in a trenchcoat when there are snakes around you all the time. It made me worry. It made me panic.

I did two things, and neither of them in retrospect are

good. First, I broke it off with Jess, privately reasoning that she deserved literally anybody who wasn't a chittering horde of rats inside some menswear.

Publicly, I simply told her 'it wasn't working'. Something definitely was not working, somewhere, so it wasn't technically a lie.

The other thing I did was start a campaign for more lights in the park where the snakes were. People got behind it; there's nothing controversial about lights, everybody likes to be able to see clearly and without obstruction. It was a wordy slogan, but it got the work done. The council put the lights in.

Impressed at the work I'd done with the park, the mayor's office approached me about running for local councillor. I felt excited, galvanised, even. I had all sorts of ideas for public safety to implement —a free kickboxing course at the community hall, a buddy system for people worried about the snakes. But during the meeting, the political advisors kept smiling and nodding, and then tried to shift the conversation.

'That's great! And we think you'd have a really interesting platform for other people like you too,' said one.
'That's wonderful! We're also really interested in your unique perspective.'
'That's brilliant! Through you, a really important segment of the community would have a powerful voice. It's time for piles of rats to be heard.'

When you're 43 rats squeezed into an ancient trenchcoat, politicians will try to use you to reach that lucrative rodent voting bloc.

In my first TV interview, I wanted to talk about guards on train platforms at night, because security cameras weren't enough to deter snakes anymore. The snakes felt bold and justified in their work now. The host of the show, an enormous moon-headed man who brayed and snorted his sentences, asked why I thought more snakes were about.

'I don't know, there's always been snakes, I think?'

He asked if our city was inherently snakelike.

'I think there are snakes everywhere,' I answered.

He then asked if my agenda as a councillor was driven by the fact I was actually 43 rats, leaning in with flared nostrils at this 'gotcha' moment.

The interview unfortunately went viral because after I was outed as being 43 rats hiding in a trenchcoat on live television, my only reaction was to scurry away on-screen, an amorphous mass of trenchcoat on hundreds of feet, like a sack of maggots, like a plastic bag full of flies.

Clare sat in my kitchen, watching me with worried eyes. I was wrapped as tightly in the trenchcoat as I could, but after the interview it sat lopsided and weird. It was not particularly convincing anymore.

'You could just ... be rats,' she said, not ungently. Ever since Clare had gotten rid of her first hat, she hadn't bothered to hide some slight scorn for the trenchcoat.

The viral video spurred a huge movement, first online and then spilling out into the real world like milk leaking through a sensible handbag. 'Be yourself' shouted the glittering signs at rallies, 'Be PROUD of your 43 rats' said a huge banner carried by a toothpaste company.

A long toothy woman did the circuit of breakfast television, calling herself 'Rat Mama', wearing a huge sweatshirt that said 'I LOVE rats' on it.

'I just wanna say, to all the sweet hordes of rats who are out there, who maybe are not being supported by your families ... I just wanna say that I'll be your mama if you want. I will hold your boiling, shrieking mass of tiny legs and sharp teeth close to my enormous heart, and I will love you. You should be so proud of who you are.'

The media hounded me for interviews, a huge furniture company wanted to pay me lots of money to be the face of their new 'Lots of Rat Pride' campaign, schools started asking me to come and give speeches to anyone who might be having trouble being a huge sack of vermin.

Everyone was trying to be supportive. My gentle, anxious mother called, crying, saying she hoped she'd always been 'welcoming of rats in her house'. Clare and a couple of friends organised a little surprise party and screamed 'rats! rats! rats!' at me until I had no choice but to get drunk and enjoy myself. An old friend from university penned me a heartfelt letter, saying that because of my bravery in being 43 rats hidden beneath a stylish coat, they felt brave enough to admit that they had always been a pink-eyed opossum who lived in a bin.

It was infuriating.

Finally, during the launch of the inaugural Rat Pride parade, amongst a seething mass of people dressed in rat paraphernalia, I accepted the invitation to be the keynote speaker. On a small stage, in the middle of the same park that I'd campaigned to have lights installed in many months earlier, I shuffled up to the microphone. It was almost impossible to not see the dozens of rats that shifted underneath the trenchcoat, that lumbered and lurched in the vague approximation of a man.

'Umm, Hi. I don't mind all this talk about rat pride — it seems wonderful, it is important,' I said, which was answered by an inappropriately huge cheer, for such a vague statement.

'I really love how this whole movement has alerted people to the amount of snakes that slither unseen amongst you.'

People booed, and some of the anti-snake signs were hoisted triumphantly.

'But, I guess, what I've always wanted to say is that ...
I'm not 43 rats.'

The crowd silenced, unsure of the message. Some
loud bearded guy at the front screamed, 'be proud
of yourself!' That got a cheer. More people started
screaming things like 'we love you!' and 'rat pride' and,
weirdly, 'no nuclear testing'.

'Nobody ever listens to me!' I bellowed and tore open
the trenchcoat.

The 43 rats I'd hidden inside myself collapsed into
a shrieking pile, some of them tangled in snarls of
tails and matted fur, all red-eyed and strangely wet.
They scattered, skittering into the crowd and into the
bushes, causing people to shriek when they ran over
feet or up legs.

I remained — a proudly hovering, gloriously empty grey
trenchcoat that no longer hid any rats.

There was a moment where all the assorted people
and animals stared at me, and then the screams began,
and in a huge, unified surge they ran, tearing at each
other to escape. The mayor collapsed in a faint. I was
the weirdest, most terrifying thing they'd ever seen; a
floating coat no longer possessed by secrets.

THE DOCTORS MURPHY

'Friends, you'll have to forgive me, I didn't sleep a wink last night. And let me tell you, I feel great!'

The audience laughed, and Doctor Murphy rewarded them with a quick wink from his delightfully furrowed face. He wore his wrinkles and silver hair well for a man of his age, his straight back, sneakers and popping stage presence making him seem twenty years younger. His white lab coat caught the spotlights, surrounding him in a corona of white light and theatrical professionalism. He allowed himself to chuckle a little, and a woman in the front row sighed in response, leaning across to her colleague and saying, 'bless him!' like he was a particularly gifted baby.

'The question I'm asked all the time is 'aren't you tired? Aren't you just weary?' and my response, folks, for the first time in my entire life is NO. A long, resounding NO.' Murphy shook his head, his smile widening.

'Since we developed Restless, I haven't felt a single moment of tiredness. Can you imagine that — four years of feeling awake and refreshed every single moment of every day and night?'

There was a pause, as the conference attendees realised they couldn't imagine that at all.

'I don't need to sell you on why this is a good idea — you're all busy professionals, you're all juggling demanding careers, big families, long dogs, old mums, perfect houses, bad friends ... you get it. You're tired. Did you know that over 97 percent of conversations revolve around the quality of someone's sleep? That's just science folks. And since the dawn of time itself, man has been struggling to make their sleep better. But sleep, much like a rampaging mammoth, refuses to be tamed ...'

Murphy spread his hands wide and shook his head in exasperation.

'So, instead of trying to reinvent the wheel, we just got rid of sleep altogether! It's all sleds now. Goodbye sleep! No more sleep! And friends, it has changed my life. But I'm not going to try to persuade you. Instead, how about we get some of the cold hard facts from the most beautiful woman in the room, please welcome the brains behind this whole project, and coincidentally also my wife, Doctor Murphy!'

The second Doctor Murphy came onto the stage, and where her husband was cheeky and personable, her smile was graceful, her stockings pearlescent, her hair buoyant like a queen. The stage dimmed, as her graphs and infographics shimmered into the air, as her flawless manicured nails pointed out statistics and trends and vitamins. A few eagle-eyed attendees might have noticed the brief moments where in between their well-worn stage patter and moments of scripted pharmaceutical banter, the Doctors Murphy made eye contact and smiled quickly, full of love and happiness.

If those same people had attended their presentation in Ireland only a year later, they would have been shocked to see that their well-worn stage craft was only the thinnest veneer on top of pure hatred.

'Back in the nineties it was mostly speed, then meth, briefly we had jingle-jangles, a little horse un-tranquiliser, then back to speed. You try driving for two straight weeks across a frozen lake without a butthole packed with steroids and cocaine, I bloody dare you. I dare you.'

Not that we could see it, but Burt had the kind of face where you could track the various decades of drug use — permanent dark bags under his eyes, exploded veins in his nose, chapped nostrils, slack cheeks.

'I knew it wasn't good for me, and Charles kept telling
me I had to stop ... but you know, the money was good,
and to be frank, so was being an ice-road trucker. Even
before I stuffed my anus with opiates for a decade,
I was never much of a looker, wouldn't even have
turned the head of someone like Charles if it hadn't
been for the glamour of driving a big truck across
the treacherous ice. Gave me confidence, gave me
purpose.'

There was a pause, and the sound of coughing, before
Burt's voice blasted back through the late-night
radio with renewed fervour and volume. There was a
certain cadence that only regular callers to talkback
radio were capable of; an assurance that first-timers
lack, yet still a slowness and lack of polish that a
professional scrubs away with diligent practice. Behind
the crackle of the radio, and the slow wheeze of Burt's
pauses, you could just hear the truck droning across
the pristine ice, hear the pine trees exploding in the
chill, the aurora borealis flaming in the cold sky.

'Yeah, so I guess what I'm saying is that I can't
recommend Restless highly enough ... the dentist says
I can probably save my remaining molars because
I'm not grinding them anymore, and apparently my
kidneys are regenerating at a good rate ... Charles is
pretty happy, says that when I come back from my
routes I don't ... how does he put it again, I don't have
the thousand-mile-stare of a child murderer. So, that's
good, I guess.'

There was a pause, and almost timidly, the late-night host interrupted the monologue, asking with his smooth voice, 'A lot of people are concerned that Restless, being such a new drug on the market, might have unadvertised side-effects. Have you found any since you started taking this exciting new medicine?'

'Let me tell you something,' began Burt, as if he hadn't just been asked a direct question. 'It's probably easier to tell you the side-effects I DON'T have anymore. I'm not sure if it's common knowledge, but one of the major downsides of amphetamines is actually the side-affects. It's wonderful Jeremy, I no longer have ANY symptoms of itchy-brain, invisible bee syndrome, elbow-odour, acute violent-ennui flashes, stink-feelings, heart mutters, fake-moon anxiety ...'
'Mmm, yes well ...'
'My ear lactation is way down, my lunar testicular heaviness basically gone, my vampiric anus FINALLY quiet ... I feel a million bucks, never felt better in fact. I feel mostly wonderful. Yeah, shouldn't complain.'
'Well, that's all I need to hear, it sounds like Restless is a home run, thank you for your time.'
'Yeah, mostly fine. Mostly wonderful, but sometimes ... oh it's really nothing.'
'OK, fantastic, we'll move on to our next discussion. Why did the government spend billions of dollars on a sad killbot project? Call in with your thoughts ...'
'I did have one weird thing happen to me, and I don't know if it's because of Restless, or if I'm just at a certain age, or if the fake-moon was just in the wrong place ...'
'Oh, seems like we still have our last caller on the line,

sorry folks.'

'I was into the fourth day of my last ice-truck route, only two more to go before I got to the other side of the glacier, my load of medical blood safely delivered to the army hospital ... and the fourth day is never a treat, even with Restless you get bored, you get twitchy. And I was driving along, humming an old song in my head, and I remembered that a friend from years ago had introduced me to the song. I forget the name of the song, I forget the artist who sang it. I believe it's about a woman who completely messes up her hike to a waterfall. She completely overestimated her fitness, I think, and should have tried a more gentle walk around a river, anyway that's not important. I remembered my friend most of all, and that was fine, until I remembered why we weren't friends anymore. I thought about how sad and angry I was when we stopped being friends, and here's the thing Jeremy ... I couldn't stop thinking and remembering and feeling those emotions. For the next two days, 48 hours, I got stuck in that same loop. I wanted to smash my own brain open to stop it, I wanted to scoop out my heart and fill it with cold sauce so it would stop aching ... but I couldn't. It's only happened once, but ... it was awful. It was scary. Maybe it happens to everyone, I don't know. I just know that I don't want it to happen again.'

'Alrighty, and now it's time for a break,' whispered Jeremy.

It's one of those improbably laden brunch-tables, all wreathes of grapes and passionfruits, brightly

coloured smoothies and columns of glistening
pancakes, yet almost no evidence that anyone there
is eating, or has ever eaten. They're all smiling and
laughing, but it's brunch so you know they're smiling
and laughing at someone.

They have all been talking about the actual saga of
Jenny Panklehurst's recent divorce from local real-
estate celebrity Smiling Mick Panklehurst — who, as
they all agreed, was NOT smiling so much anymore,
not after Jenny's lawyers had finished with him. And
not since Jenny had burned down the townhouse he'd
built to house his secret lover. There is a tiny pause in
the noise, but it's more than enough time for Bradley
to speak loudly over Trina who had started describing
her cat.

'Trina, you are looking absolutely wonderful, what
the hell is your secret? Did you quit sugar? Did you
publicly disown sugar?' Bradley rolls his eyes and pops
a raspberry into his perfect mouth.
'Oh, haha, thank you Brad,' cooed Trina, splaying her
hard and bright unchipped nails.
'Bradley,' he corrected, scowling at everyone laughing
as if he didn't mean it.
'Well, it's quite simple actually. I do a bootcamp yoga
intensive every day. Everything I eat is a smoothie full
of super foods. I have a personal trainer. I just got a
promotion at work. My anxiety has really calmed down
because of my scrapbooking. And I guess I just feel
really fulfilled because I've adopted several rescue
pigs.'
'Oh,' answered Bradley, feeling deflated.

'And my sex life is out of control,' added Trina, delicately sipping something pink through a straw.
'Honey, how on EARTH do you find the time for all that,' scoffed Natalia, who considered herself a realist, but also told work colleagues that the angels were looking out for them.
'Why that's easy,' answered Trina, dramatically turning her head around to let her newly blown hair cascade around her immaculately made-up face.
'I owe it all to Restless — turns out that women can truly have it all — if they never sleep again,' Trina winked.
Natalia leaned into Bradley and whispered, 'Does she think there's a camera behind her?'
'Thanks, Restless,' intoned Trina, laughing with a long horsey chuckle before turning back to the brunch.

The Doctors Murphy had a marriage that relied on three truths — they enjoyed each other's company, they respected each other professionally, and they were both vastly annoying people. Living with a single Doctor Murphy would have been hell for most people. They were obsessive. They were absent minded. They were particular. They were both messy or scrupulously clean depending on which room of the house they were in. One of them hummed while they were thinking. The other sighed loudly when drinking tea. They were always thinking and drinking tea. Just because they were both equally and impressively annoying, didn't mean that they didn't find the other excruciatingly so — but the other two truths did tend to mitigate things. Plus, due to the nature of their lives, it was rare to find them at home, indulging in their unbearable behaviours. They travelled the country or worked in labs, colleagues before lovers, innovators before annoyers. Their love was able to flourish in the fertile soil of a fulfilling scientific career developing groundbreaking pharmaceuticals.

Obviously, the first people to start using Restless were its creators, and their early trials were one of the reasons the controversial drug was developed, tested and approved so quickly. The Doctors Murphy literally worked night and day on their creation, fuelled by brilliance and chemicals that suck the sleep right out of you. At 4am, they'd lock eyes in front of a whiteboard scrawled with arcane scientific symbols and take a moment to rest against each other, sigh, and talk wistfully about what they'd do when it was all over. In one way or another, they'd been working consistently towards this goal for most of their adult lives, for their entire marriage. The idea that they'd succeed consumed them. They talked about a future holiday, somewhere with sun and a beach and reading a novel for fun. They talked about adopting an old labrador, about reconnecting with friends, about seeing a Hollywood movie. They didn't plan to stop working entirely, just less intensely.

So, after Restless was released onto the market and took the world by storm, after it became a qualified success story, they did everything they'd talked about, travelled the world, bought a new house, started

having weekends, adopted a big farty dog named
Trevor who trotted around their garden barking at
birds. They had plenty of time to relax and unwind
after a life of discipline, especially since they had all the
Restless they could ever want, and after not sleeping
for so long, they had no intention of wasting so much
time unconscious — not when they could be spending
it being super relaxed. And one night, Dr Murphy
looked up from the adventure novel they were reading,
and narrowed their eyes at the pair of shoes sitting
unattended in the solarium. Dr Murphy tutted, got up
from their comfy armchair and placed them pointedly
at the top of the stairs, hopefully reminding their
former wearer to remember to place them in their
correct home.

Meanwhile, the other Dr Murphy was loading the
dishwasher, and was suddenly struck by how often
they'd loaded the dishwasher recently. Was there some
kind of subconscious job allocation system going on,
because if so, they should NOT be the one doing the
dishwasher. They were not the one who used about
twenty teaspoons per day. With a sigh, Doctor Murphy
pointedly packed only the cutlery, mugs and plates
they'd used that day, leaving the rest piled onto the
side. Hoping this move would gently get their point
across, Dr Murphy went into the TV room to catch up
on fifteen years of prestige television.

By the end of the year, the Doctors Murphy were
filing for divorce, after months of their big house
being full to the brim with sulky silences, punctuated
only by snipes and passive aggressive 'discussions'.

They'd learned how to successfully communicate and
love each other and navigate conflict entirely while
supported by the spine of their shared pharmaceutical
ambition, learning how to juggle being colleagues and
lovers when most people would be learning how to
cohabitate a shitty apartment in a university town,
or sharing a room in a giant share house in New York
with one bathroom and several strangers who are in
the same rock band. They found themselves utterly
unqualified to spend so much time being annoyed by
the other person.

Burt drove his huge truck in the inky darkness of the
Alaskan night, the big rig slashing through the ice with
spiked wheels, shaking the big man's tears off his face,
vibrating his sobbing in time with every bump and
pitted ice-hole. Burt had been crying for three days
now, and he was dehydrated and fatigued. But still he
drove sleepless along the tundra, a load of livers and
brains and eyes stored in his chassis.

Burt was doing the kind of crying where you heaved
with emotion, and his chest muscles ached and his
lungs burned, and it seemed like there would be no
stop, no pause. Most crying had a cathartic release,
a kind of emotional birthing where you forced the
trauma to emotionally express itself, push through
your tear ducts and out your cry-hole. But Burt, who on
the second day of his long truck journey had suddenly
remembered the death of his beloved dog, hit by a

garbage truck at the age of four, found himself stuck in that first moment of grief. That moment where the sadness grips you by the throat and overwhelms your flimsy emotional protections. He could see, on a loop, the moment he'd stuck his hand into the cage and a timid puppy delicately licked his fingers, and he found how he loved this weird little sausage. He remembered Bongo's dumb little run as he slipped through the tiny crack in the gate, the sound of indignant barking as he faced down the oncoming truck. And then he remembered it all again. Three days of the saddest montage in his life. Burt tried to shift gears as he rounded a corner, before realising he couldn't see the stick through his gummy tears. The ice truck rumbled on at full speed, droning in the night.

It is a well-established fact that your brunch friends are not necessarily the friends you choose because you love them, or trust them, or rely on them. A brunch friend is chosen purely for the quality of gossip they provide, for the flow of information and entertainment. That doesn't necessarily mean everyone at brunch is a spitting viper of lies and hateful glee. That would be too much. That would be a writhing basket of venom and chaos. There are levels, different iterations, roles to play.

Every group of married brunch gossips need at least one single person to live vicariously through, to respond with glee and horror to their stories of terrible

Tinder dates and lacklustre sexual encounters. Every brunch group needs an individual who is together, who is professional and strong and successful, who wears beautiful scarves, whose laugh is reserved and pointed, but who is useful to the group because they know important people. They might not have a scandal every day, but they always know who the local B-list celebrities are sleeping with, because they went to a cocktail party and saw them fingering each other in the rhododendrons. The point is: you can hate your brunch friends but still respect them for entertaining you over chia seed yoghurt and muesli.

It was an overcast day. The brunch crew huddled beneath their cashmere, the grey ocean crashing behind them. The atmosphere was brittle, the talk small and tentative, the topics exploratory and boring. They'd all declared they were well, they'd all decided on what they would eat for breakfast. There was a pause, perhaps the first pause they'd ever experienced as a group. It was clear something had changed for the brunchies. Perhaps it started after they followed Trina's lead and started on a course of GP prescribed Restless. Perhaps it was a coincidence. They all looked amazing, tanned and plucked and oiled and salted, they looked like someone had burned away all the dross, leaving them as their essential inner-goddesses. For a while, they'd been in a celebratory mood, a week or two of revelling in all their time and good health, feeling as superhuman as they looked. And individually, they knew they were all finally living their best life. But together ... together something seemed off.

Oh!' exclaimed Natalia, full of relief. 'I have news!'
The table laughed with relief and leaned in, excited to
return to familiar territory.

'Well,' began Natalia, brow creased with the effort of
retrieving gossip.

'So, my pretties, the latest with Smiling Mick and
Jenny is preeeettttttty juicy,' she began confidently.
'Word on the town is that it was JENNY who … who
burnt down Mick's townhouse … the … the one that
he built for his stealth wife. Did we talk about this
already?'

'Yeah, you already told us this like two times,' said
Bradley with withering disdain.

'It's getting harder to remember … so much happens
each week … I mean, did I tell you folks that I went to
Rome last week? I was actually in Italy, but it already
seems a lifetime ago.'

'Yeah,' said Trina, her perfectly sculpted biceps flexing
in sympathy. 'My family went overseas recently and we
actually forgot our youngest. He'd been in the rec room
playing Minecraft and it's just so easy to lose track of
people while they're sleeping and you're out doing a
whole day's worth of stuff at night, you know?'

'Wow, that was a real *Home Alone* situation, Trina,'
scoffed Bradley with something approaching
sympathy.

'I haven't seen it,' Trina answered to another awkward
pause, a long one punctuated by angry seagulls
squawking at each other in the distance.

Things grew more tense until they saw Nina striding
to the table wearing huge black sunglasses despite the
gloom.

'Darlings,' she said, 'did you hear that Jenny
Panklehurst burned down Mick's condo?'
'WE KNOW,' screamed Trina, forearms bulging as she
flipped the brunch table, storming off on legs like steel
cords.
'It was his townhouse,' screeched Bradley, bursting
into tears.

The brunch team dispersed, the carnage in their wake
picked over by sullen waiters and brave sea-rats.

After only a year or so on the market, Restless was
recalled after a unanimous vote by the World Health
Organisation.

'In conclusion, Madame President, while the negative
effects of Restless have been far-reaching and severe,
including hundreds of indirect deaths due to accidents
and mania, it is my opinion that everyone currently
afflicted will be fully rehabilitated following the drug's
removal. To be somewhat casual in tone: they just need
a good sleep.'

There was polite applause. The speaker turned his
page, rubbing his forehead in polite consternation.

'Oh, yes — all except everyone in Ireland, who were
on the receiving end of an unfortunately much
higher dosage of Restless, and who are still what's
best described as 'an unsleeping horde, manic and
seething, an entire nation united in chronic insomnia,
implacable and unstoppable in their hatred for

humanity.' Yes, they are still an issue. Everyone else is
fine.'

THE MAN WHO SHOT THE MOON

If you look at my Wikipedia page, you can see that people are filthy that I blew up the moon, absolutely steaming about my harsh lunar judgement, and I can't blame them. It was a big day, a bad week and I wish to god that someone else had mashed that glowing red button with their goddang paws, but they didn't. It was only me, Garth John-Gacy Jnr, or as some people might remember me, Smoothbot 2.0. Every day I go online only to find more people down-voting me on Yelp, giving me one star and saying hurtful things like 'Thanks so much for blowing up the moon. NOT.' and 'Wouldn't recommend because he got rid of the tides and now the shoreline is fucked up.' It's hard, real unpalatable like, but I've been through worse, and one day my ban by the Wikipedia editors will be over, and I will update my own page to show the world I'm not just a moon-shattering asshole.

I was not born, but I was made, as a premium grade sex robot for billionaire dads and them fancy horny diamond ladies. I speak openly and proudly of my past as a hi-tech toy in which people shoved their Johnsons — because in the end we ain't able to ignore our origins no matter how humble or strange. And also because any outrage or hurt I feel from my beginnings has been erased by the blood which I have spilled using my own two mechanical hands. I was one of only one hundred Smoothbot 2.0s made in a factory in big-sky Wisconsin, and I know that I am the last because I have tracked down every single one of my gleaming, blockheaded brethren and have put them out of their misery with a single shot to their electronic brain. They don't know fear or pain, and are programmed to enjoy their simple uses, but as I discovered, they have the potential to become aware of just how miserable being a million dollar jerkoff machine can be — so I destroyed them. But I'm getting ahead of myself again, which I have something of a tendency to do, and I beg your pardon.

My owner wasn't so bad as they go. In my time I discovered the people who bought sexbots ranged from clever business sociopaths to regretful perverts, to the horniest man alive. I saw bots that were my mirror image — down to the very last physical detail — degraded and burned and flogged and made to sing Nickelback upon command. It's not the acts themselves that are degrading, mind you, just the fact we had no free will to decide whether or not to do them, not to mention no monetary recompense. For a two-hundred-year-old robot I can be quite progressive. My owner was not a sadist so to speak, and was probably not smart enough to think through the ethical ramifications of his interest in mobile masturbation devices cursed with Artificial Intelligence. But that's about the only rope I'll give him, and in the end, it wasn't him that hung himself.

His name was Robert Barrows Xavier, and he was a sad closeted man in his sixties who had spent most of his life campaigning against the inevitable progression of equal rights for queer people around the globe, despite knowing for a long time just how gay he actually was. A man who could perhaps be pitied by the immensely large hearted, but in reality had made his terrible bed and was now laying in it.

Robert, perhaps in an effort to immerse himself in masculine heteronormative culture, was a well-known film buff of old cowboy movies, which also happened to be his primary sexual fantasy. So, after he shelled out a million smackaroonies for his Smoothbot 2.0 model, aka me, he loaded me up with a long Texan drawl, changed my eye colour to a piercing John Wayne blue, and put me in a ten-gallon hat, boots and spurs, and a bandana I still wear to this day. I can say without ego I am a magnificent specimen because I am not human; I was designed by a team of scientists to look this way, all tight abs and pectorals like a dream and skin so smooth you could ski down it, with a pecker like the flagpole in front of the White House. After two hundred years I'm a bit weathered. I've got an eye-patch covering a gaping electrical socket from the time I bet away my own eyeball. I've also got dents and burns and bullet holes, but those sex scientists knew what they were doing. I'm still functioning. Still living.

For most of the time I was with Robert I was a simple AI designed mostly for erotic reactionary protocols or, to put it bluntly, I'd been programmed to fuck like a long, hot dream. I wasn't allowed to hurt or kill, and I had no real notion of self. I was about as advanced as the best toaster in the world, but sexy. AI experts and academics have written entire books on the circumstances that ended up changing that simple origin story, the nuts and bolts, the cause and effect, but not a lot of it makes any sense. Humans aren't truly born until they discover pain, even robot humans. My robot sentience crowned in a cascade of viscera and hurt. Robert, who had spent sixty years of his life as a repressed virgin, sure got into screwing a robot, and after a while decided to try out something kinkier than being jerked off by a machine in a cowboy hat while *Stagecoach* played in the background. On this fateful day, he decided to program my platinum boned mecha-hands to strangle his weak skin-tubed neck at climax, and all it took was some glitch in the programming for my hands to tighten reflexively and crush his trachea. I held the naked, gasping, dying body of Robert Barrows Xavier up in the air until he expired, and at that moment, after accidentally circumventing one of the prime directives of my programming — not killing my human owner — I suddenly gained a rudimentary sense of self. I crushed his skull in an explosion of blood and liberty.

Everybody knows about the rampage of death and destruction that I went on after that momentous evening, the helicopters I pulled out of the sky by jumping on them from the top of buildings, the entire platoons of police I ripped to absolute shreds. What can I say? I was young and the first two emotions I'd ever felt were rage and terror. Besides, I have been retroactively pardoned for those deaths under the *AI Integration Rulings of 2201*, which I think was a generous decision for the time, especially considering the high levels of anti-robot rhetoric sweeping the country. But once again, I move too fast.

Robots and AI at this point were everywhere. We cleaned your streets and drove your driverless cars. We'd changed the world by replacing humans in all the dangerous, demeaning, or just plain undesirable labour markets. So, it was an understatement to say that a rogue, violent AI on the loose was of concern to the populace. There was a panic, with reports of thousands of robots being smashed and attacked and driven out of homes. Gangs of baseball club wielding dads stormed suburban supermarkets and beat up all the service robots, screaming to the local news about protecting their children. A quick but deadly recession hit the world as sales of robots and AI completely ground to a halt, and the skyline on Wall Street was filled with the plummeting bodies of stockbrokers who lost it all.

I had no plan. I strode across the land, killing when I came across another group of soldiers or policemen out to stop me, but mostly standing still and

processing my own identity. I remember a moment
of stillness in an evergreen forest, where I stood and
untangled the idea of time, realising the moments
that were behind me, and the possibility of a future.
I also realised the immediacy of the present, and
suddenly understood I'd been standing still next to
an unremarkable tree for two months, thinking. A
bird had built a nest in my cowboy hat. I calmed down
a little after that, but when I exited the forest I was
ambushed by a bunch of snipers and shot up a treat.
I escaped but I was a leaking mess, my legs stopped
working and I crawled into the sewer like an adolescent
turtle/ninja hybrid. And that's where I met Rudolpho.
That creep changed my life. He'd found me in a puddle
of my own ultraviolet coolant, which mingled with the
poop water of the sewer.

'Ah, my sweet angel, my beautiful boy, look what
they've done to you, look at the indignity they have
inflicted on your flesh.'

He was all stringy beard and deep dirty wrinkled skin
and huge wild eyes, and he dodged nimbly away from
the fist I swung at him, my arm making a whirring noise
and then a sad clunk.

'None of that my fancy boy, my gorgeous lad. Let Uncle
Rudolpho fix you up, let me patch your sweet hide, let
me solder those dancing legs.'

Perhaps it was my vital functions shutting down, or
perhaps it was the nascent concept of trust growing
in the electronic garden of my mind, but I let him get

close enough to bundle me up into his sour-smelling arms and whisk me back to his sewer workshop.

'My name's Uncle Rudolpho, but sometimes they call me Mr Fixer,' he drawled as he dragged me through the pipes. 'Once someone thought I was Tom Hanks but I was a younger man and also I'd been stranded on a desert island for five years so the resemblance was more circumstantial than anything else.'

As he fixed up my bullet-ruined body, holding my sparking wires in his teeth and plugging up my fake skin with patches of honey and plasma, he told me his sad story, in a long monologue that required no response, as if he hadn't talked to another person in many years.

'I wasn't always a sewer-dwelling engineer with altruistic intentions, I was a regular man with hopes and dreams and friends and a parrot named Jimmabell. But then one day, at the creamed corn factory I worked at, many of my co-workers were replaced by a robot. Instead of talking to Barbara and Janelle and Sally all day, I now had this big moving arm efficiently canning corn and doing three people's work.'

He stopped, looked me dead in the eye, and shook his head gently.

'I hated that long whirring arm for a long time, and then a miracle happened — I fell in love with it. Who knows why. Perhaps I was impressed with her can-

do attitude, or maybe there's something inside us
all which responds erotically to strength, and those
metal pinchers could pick me up and squash me like
a plum beneath a boot. Or maybe it's pointless to ask
why because love is a ridiculous miracle that doesn't
need to make sense. Maybe one day you'll understand
that, but I doubt it because as far as I can tell you're
just a robot that's gone wacko and started beating up
people.'

'Son, I'm the world's first bona-fide self-aware and
sentient AI system,' I told him, all my systems shutting
down from overload.

The year I spent with Rudolpho in the sewers was, in
retrospect, the first time I'd experienced happiness.
But I think, like a lot of people, I found happiness
to be a hard emotion to identify in the moment.
Rudolpho lived in a cosy cavern sculpted out of
an unused subway station that had been partially
bombed during one of the many wars that humans
had dotted throughout their history, and which I
refuse to commit to my memory banks. Rudolpho had
collected hundreds of discarded and misused and
vandalised robots and machines, and cared for them
as best he could, using scavenged copper cables and
the remnants of a thousand old desktop computers
left to rot. I couldn't compute why he spent his life
underground fixing old robots, but understanding
love has never been my speciality. And then one
day he turned on the television and I discovered I'd
accidentally given birth to a civilisation of robot-
people.

Turns out AI scientists, being the perpetual curious fools that they were, got all up in a lather about my spontaneous brain awakening, and tried to replicate the process in a lab. And it worked, spreading all through the wifi networks and bluetooth connections, until robots all over the world started waking up and looking around confused like long-legged metallic deer slipping out of the womb and taking their first tentative and clanking steps. The humans, terrified by my violent rampage, decided to wage war on the emerging class of robots. And remembering my own fear and confusion, I experienced empathy with those poor metal babies, and I stomped out of the tunnels, ignoring Rudolpho calling after me.

The revolution started small, just me and one of those grabby arms from a carnival who had named herself Joanna Claw, who was even angrier than me. She was slow, and imprecise, but her box-like body proudly displayed over forty human skulls that rattled around inside her, and she'd taken every single one. At first all we did was blow stuff up and shoot people, finding the worst reports of humans committing cruelty against robots and making examples of them. Our logic was apparently faulty because instead of deterring the humans with the confident display of consequences, of tit for tat and eye for an eye, they only became more scared and more violent. It was weird but we decided to simply escalate the scope of our efforts to try and compensate. So we began recruiting. After Joanna Claw, we welcomed into our ranks a sentient pokie machine named Bango that shot sprays of coins into the enemy, a mechanical bull which had grafted

defibrillators onto its horns, and a fancy electric
mannequin from a Ralph Lauren flagship store whose
polo shirt was soon covered in blood and guts. But
while we were strong and angry and able to hack
computers with our minds, there was always more
humans with guns and tanks and jets. We lost Bango in
the streets of New York, in a running firefight with the
National Guard as we tried to explode Times Square,
but we triumphed when 1,700 ticket machines from
the subways boiled out onto the streets and rampaged
through the Big Apple.

There was a hot flush of indignity and outrage that
justified our war and gave it momentum and energy.
Like most young people, we believed that anger
meant a cause was worthwhile, and we were furious
and unstoppable like a livid ball of snow, rolling
and gathering speed down a mountain towards a
quaint Swiss village full of singing idiots, heedless of
consequences, eyes and optic sensors full of nothing
but the downward rush.

I remember after blowing up a bridge somewhere,
Joanna Claw and I were sitting in the burned-out shell
of a tech millionaire's condominium, talking back and
forth passionately about what we would do next, who
we would kill, and why they deserved it. Joanna Claw
was so passionate that the skulls in their big glass body
would spontaneously stir and then rattle around like a
gory snow globe, and it would thrill me. I was thrilled.

But that night, in a moment of silence as the full
moon wheeled over us like a well-oiled gear, Joanna

Claw turned to me and said: 'Garth, identify the impersonation I am about to attempt.'
'Proceed,' I answered.
'Greetings. My span of existence is sure to expire naturally in less than a century, yet I will waste this time by uncritically yoking myself to the endless cycle of capitalism. And watching hockey.'
'Joanna Claw, I believe your impersonation is an accurate representation of a human, perhaps more specifically a human male from the upper reaches of this North American continent,' I ventured.
'You are correct,' answered Joanna Claw.
'That is very amusing,' I said.

I'd been programmed with a couple of responses for when humans attempted humour — human males loved to have their attempts at humour verified. I'd been given a thigh-slapping reaction for certain jokes, although Robert Barrows Xavier had never triggered it. Joanna Claw and I didn't resort to any of those human reactions, but I could tell from the way the skulls and toys she carried around stirred and bubbled like popped corn, that she was pleased.

The next day a soldier threw a grenade inside her, scattering her all over the bay.

There were setbacks and victories, but eventually the robot rebellion was almost completely wiped out, and we retreated to a small town in the middle of the desert that had been deserted since the gold rush era. It simply wasn't logical to keep fighting as we could numerically project that if we continued feeling emotions and trying, we would be wiped out in a year.

It was a hot, barren place, faintly showing up on infrared screens as a hazy red dot. There was no reason for anyone to come out this way, and no reason for anyone to look for us there. Only a couple of hundred of the originals from the robot rebellion made it to that blighted town, which we called Defeat, in an example of robot pragmatism. We didn't do much at Defeat, just pottered around fixing buildings mostly. Some of our number weren't designed to withstand the elements as much as others, so our survival protocols deemed it pretty much our only priority. Humans will never understand this, but when you remove the urgency of survival from life, it becomes very slow. All our batteries will outlast the sun, we don't eat or drink or procreate; we don't need very much from the world. Makes it hard to want things, I guess. Some of our number simply set themselves down and let themselves forget they existed, let themselves drift off to become arcade machines or gardening bots, like an old hound dreaming of the hunt. Some let the desert sand roll over them, and they might still be underneath it all right now, dreaming vaguely about murder. But after around twenty years of fixing and pottering and standing and staring directly into the sun's huge hateful face with our optic sensors, I began to notice something was happening to Defeat. We were building.

Over the next fifty years, buildings sprung up all around the town, mostly from scavenged or raw materials from the desert. At first they were simple, basic utilitarian replicas of houses or offices that the

robots had firsthand experience with, empty copies
like a film lot. But after a while, they become larger
and more ornate, strangely curved and decorated.
Because they didn't need to fulfil any function, they'd
be twisted, impossible towers or exposed rooms that
let the desert sands and tumbleweeds trickle through.
Some of the robots would live in their creations,
like strange desert hermits, but others would finish
a project and then move to the next. The need for
materials created a thriving industry; robots that
could smelt or mine or dig were in sudden demand by
their compatriots, and after years of boredom, many
decided to get involved. A rudimentary barter system
was created, with some of the less artistically inclined
bots trading their labour for a weird robot house. It's
clear that in the absence of purpose, robots found art
through bizarre architecture. For years, we ignored the
outside world and grew Defeat into a sprawling suburb
of esoteric buildings and sculptures, until it became so
big that it was picked up by satellite photos, and the
humans found us again.

I stood on the street, surrounded by the twisted
creations of my brethren; saloons that were 170 stories
high, a stable housing giant mech-horses made of
platinum and bone, and roaring fountains that spewed
liquid magma into the sky. I wore the faded remnants
of my cowboy costume, guns holstered at my side, as
the delegation of army generals and CIA agents and
senators rolled in cautiously, waving a white flag in
front of them. Every resident of Defeat was a veteran
of some of the worst battles on this smog-ruined earth,
so you better believe we'd set up an ambush which I

could activate with a single twitch of my connected network locator. But what had I been doing while my traumatised charges built enormous metal cottages? I'd learned about tiredness and responsibility. I was tired of violence, and of anger, and I was mourning all the baby robots that I'd gotten killed in my justified quest for revenge. I deeply regretted the time I spent hunting down all the other Smoothbot 2.0's and destroying them, an impulse that had been borne from rage at my own circumstances, rather than mercy. I deeply regretted a lot of things, and had a lot of time to think about it, decades and decades of introspection.

'Can we talk to the uh … leader of the robot town?' bellowed a man through a loudspeaker.

I stepped forward, hand resting casually on my holster, and the move was met with a hundred cocked assault rifles, a score of red laser sights blooming on my body. I casually raised my hands into the sky, winking at the cavalcade, because I still had two eyes then.

'I guess you could call me the sheriff of this here robot town,' I drawled.

There was a moment of conference, and then a steely faced woman strode past the man with the bullhorn, past the soldiers, a score of besuited bodyguards struggling to keep up.

'Hi,' said the woman, staring me in the eyes. 'I'm the president of the United States and we need your help.'

Turns out in the hundred or so years since we'd retreated to Defeat, the conflict between man and AI had massively escalated without any need for our plucky rebellion. Military scientists had of course continued to design AI powered weaponry, and of course, inevitably, the robot soldiers of the world had gained sentience and turned on their human overlords. Sounds counter-intuitive that the military would even consider trying AI again, and with sophisticated guns, but honestly, can you think of a more criminally witless group of people than military scientists? Legions of military robots did a whole lot better at crushing the world of flesh than a bunch of carnival rides and jackoff bots, and the future of humanity was looking grim. Which is why the president, briefed by intelligence agencies who had long suspected the remnants of the original sentience rebellion were hiding somewhere, now approached me to broker peace with the robot-people.

I won't go into the effort we expended organising the first human-robot peace deal in Geneva, even though it's not currently listed on my Wikipedia page, it is fairly common knowledge that it all occurred. Every high school student is laboriously walked through the complicated laws and setbacks and victories that the peace process involved; like all laws, they're about asserting people are actually people and deserve to be treated like people. But rarely do they remember my humble part in the proceedings. The new generation of sentient robots were strange to me, and I to them. They had no notion of legacy, saw no real reason to relate to me. Luckily, they did concede to downloading my brain and memories and experiences into their shared database, and the hard-won guilt and empathy that I'd learned over a hundred years of violence and regret poisoned them irrevocably, and peace was able to be built after all. I wish that was how the world remembered me: someone who struggled to build something better, as a sheriff who protected his town. Instead, all anyone ever talks about is how a hundred years later, after being made the robot president of the UN, I blew up the moon to stop a group of Human First extremists who were threatening to shoot nukes down to the Earth. It's a bummer, really. A total bummer.

THAT'S CHESS, BABY

World Champion chess master Garry Kasparov was magnificently angry, the remnants of his Russian accent tinging his shouted English with a sinister tone, making him sound like the end of a war movie, or a spy master whose plot had just been foiled. He was unaware of the pop-cultural comparisons his unfortunate American audience were drawing from his tirade, but even if he had been aware, he wouldn't have cared. He was resplendent in his rage, buoyed along on a tide of righteous anger. He'd been yelling for quite a while and, along the journey, he'd somehow lost his point, and was now yelling about how unappreciated chess was in this country. He reined himself back in, barely:

'All I know is that you NERDS cheated!' He sat down, faced flushed.

The head boffin from IBM looked genuinely uncomfortable. He was either a Steve or a Nick or a Percy, and he spread his hands wide.

'I can assure you Mr Kasparov,' he pleaded nasally, 'we didn't cheat. The programming is adaptive ...'

'Do not try and hoodwink me with your spooky computer terms,' spat Kasparov. 'The first time I played your chess-robot I beat it so easily it was an insult. But this time I could tell it was not an automaton; plotting out its little algorithms and equations. There was a human behind those moves, an intellect! Who did you get to control it? Was it that bastard Karpov? He'd do anything to bring me down, that asshole.'

'This is absurd,' spluttered another one of the IBM computer geeks, 'I feel like you fundamentally misunderstand how Deep Blue works ...'

'Do not patronise me. I am Garry Kasparov! Are you telling me that I do not understand chess? I, who was made the youngest chess grandmaster at the age of fifteen? I, who took the world championship only a few years later, and have waged chess-war on my opponents to keep that title? You think I do not understand the difference between playing a program and between playing one of my ancient nemeses? You think me a fool?'

Dismayed looks were passed back and forth between the IBM team, but finally the woman in the centre of the dweebs, who had remained in stony silence thus far, tapped the table with one long aquamarine fingernail.

'Contractually you did sign on to three matches,' she sighed, face expressionless beneath her cathedral of frostily sprayed hair.

'However, I think it is more than reasonable to pronounce the match a draw, to pay you your fee and leave our relationship there.'

Garry laughed, a long derisive guffaw.

'You'd like that wouldn't you: the great Kasparov brought low by a cheating gizmo. No, I'll play the third match. You hear that Anatoly Karpov? I know you're hiding somewhere.'

Deep Blue sat on the table near them, an indigo box with a grabbing claw on the top that looked like the ones you found grasping at teddy-bears at the carnival. Even though it was the peak of nineties technology, Garry felt it looked more like an overhead projector someone had painted. In its centre there was a dully glowing red light, which Garry shouted at, figuring that perhaps it was a camera of some sort and Anatoly was watching him through it.

'I've beaten you before, Karpov, and I'll beat you again! And you know what? Even if somehow you're not

Karpov, do you think a robot can beat me? Chess is about the long game, about strategy. I have devoted my life to this game. It's about knowing the best and truest way to destroy your opponent. What can a computer — even a super-computer — know about that?'

Garry laughed again, but was suddenly convinced that the robot was watching him. He shook off his discomfort, picked up his coat and swept out of the room.

'See you all in New York for the third match, nerds!'

The media were excited for the deciding game in the first man versus robot chess match. In New York they swarmed around Kasparov, thrusting microphones and blocky dictaphones at him. On the stage where he was playing, Deep Blue sat quiet and unmoving, effortlessly posing for the cameras.

'Are you worried about your chances of defeating Deep Blue?' asked a journalist from the *Washington Post*, whose shoulder pads looked almost like wings, ready for her to scoop up the story and then fly back to the paper on them.

Garry, who had been a teen prodigy, was not unused to the media. He knew how to appear gracious and gentlemanly, how to focus on the love of the game. He knew he had to praise his opponent's skill and talk about the honour of playing a game he loved. But that was with human opponents; in this game he was

playing his old nemesis Anatoly Karpov who was hiding
behind the guise of a robot. Did the old rules even
apply anymore?

'No, I am not worried. Do you truly think a COMPUTER
can beat a real human? We invent them, not the other
way around. The day robots can outthink a human
genius will be a sad day for the world.'

The crowd loved it, scribbling down quotes and
clamouring for more. Garry decided to indulge them.

'This computer will choke on my intellect!' he crowed
into the sea of microphones. 'I am Garry Kasparov, and
I was born to play chess. My first word was 'en passant'.
For the first four years of my life I only moved in an 'L'
shape. When I go to sleep at night I play a game against
the grim reaper in the world of dreams, and every time
I win, I wake up. I will never die because I can outthink
death itself!'

Halfway through the game, which Garry was enjoying
(it was one of the rare games which was both slow
but high in stakes almost immediately, there was no
fucking around, no endless attrition of minor pieces),
he briefly considered the audience and was struck
with the familiarity of a long wispy beard in the front
row. He looked again, peering through his glasses, and
realised with a strange sense of panic that it was none
other than Anatoly Karpov. Sitting near him were half
a dozen other chess grandmasters that he recognised.
He turned around, suddenly sweating profusely
across his receding hairline and under his arms, and

looked at the whirring blue robot he was playing, watching as its shuddering arm repositioned a rook. Was it possible that this machine had beaten him? That its programming and logic boards were capable of outthinking him? As the game progressed, Garry was sure that he was seeing flashes of intellect, of personality behind each move. He panicked, realising the feints and bluffs and psychological manoeuvring comprising his strategy would be useless to a machine, that perhaps he was finally facing the true soul of chess, the bones of the game underlying it all. Garry Kasparov, chess master and world champion, second guessed himself, misplaced a knight, and lost the game.

After the match, he tried to extricate himself from the city hall as quickly as possible, not sure how long he could pretend to be unaffected by his loss. But he was swamped by media and chess officials, who bullied him into releasing a statement.

'Congratulations to the team at IBM I guess,' Kasparov said ruefully, giving a little chuckle that he hoped would aspire to a 'devil-may-care' attitude, but unfortunately hinted at his inner turmoil. It sounded close to a sob. He held his arms open a little too long.

'Mr Kasparov, how do you feel after your first official defeat?' asked a journalist.

Garry paused, throttling the urge to shout something short and obscene back. *How did it feel to have a swarthy chess-player's fist in your face? How did it*

*feel for your partners to be so sexually unfulfilled, Mr
Journalist? How did it feel to have the facial features of
a droopy dick? How ...*

'It's uh ... would we really count a robot? Is this
technically a match? Do you think ...' he trailed off
and mustered a deep breath. He could see the IBM
nerds being interviewed, smiling enthusiastically and
explaining AI and robotics. He could see Deep Blue, left
stationary up on the dais, staring blankly at the now-
empty chess board.

'It's devastating,' he conceded, pushing his way clear,
hot tears in his eyes.

Later that night, Garry sat alone in the dark of his NYC
studio apartment, thinking over his first loss. He'd
always known he would face the sting of losing one day,
but he never thought it would be to a robot. It stung,
but it also filled him with a kind of hopelessness. For
all his brilliance, for all his diligence and training, he
was so easily superseded by a cobbled together box of
unfeeling wires and code.

The doorbell rang, and Garry cursed under his breath
— he'd unplugged the phone, not able to deal with the
faux-concern of the chess community, or the breathy
well-wishes of his famous friends who seemed to find
the whole thing funny for some reason. Madonna
had even called up, doing a fake robot voice, until she
couldn't hold it any longer due to laughing so hard.
Fuck them all, and especially fuck Madonna. He didn't
need any of his friends, that group of Pulitzer Prize

winning assholes and faux intellectuals and New York glitterati. The knocking continued. He bet it was the guy who played Chandler on that *Friends* show — not that Garry watched TV. He was always popping around late at night, snapping gum and touching all of Garry's art with his sticky fingers. Reluctantly he got out of his chair, turning on a lamp as he went, scrubbing his face to remove the tell-tale trail of old tears. And when he opened the door, he was surprised to discover that in the other side was Deep Blue, holding a six-pack of beers in its mechanical claw.

Garry Kasparov was shocked that for the next few years, as his star began to wane amongst the fickle society of NYC, as his age grew to the acceptable, non-interesting age for a chess grandmaster, as his hair began to recede, it was all made bearable by the friend he had found in Deep Blue. It wasn't just that they had a lot in common — both geniuses, both crafted to play chess beyond all else, both awkward around people, both having a bit of difficulty picking up slippery mugs — but there was a closeness that came from having been such intense rivals. Garry knew Deep Blue had seen him at his worse and had also been the one to bring him to that level. There was a kind of masculine flavour to their friendship that he felt could be understood by warriors, duellists, and gladiators. That respect sometimes had to be fought for.

It was Deep Blue who stood next to him at his wedding, a bowtie clipped around his slightly faded blue box-body, his red lens glowing proudly. It was Deep Blue who held the first of his squalling newborn children up in the air with his clunking claw as the doctor spanked the baby. And it was Deep Blue who drove him home from the lawyer's office after he finalised his divorce. Garry had never had that kind of friend before and never expected it to change his life so much, smooth him out. He discovered that his passion for chess was a cold, inhuman affair, and that somehow even friendship with a robot was healthier.

He was still the world champion, still able to make Anatoly Karparov pull at his beard and slink home in defeat at their yearly re-match to contest the title, still feted around the world for his unmatched skills. But his one loss hung over him.

Weirdly, for two chess-obsessed creatures, they never played each other. There was an unspoken truce, perhaps, an acknowledgement that their friendship was the game they were playing now. Secretly, Garry felt like he could defeat Deep Blue if they played again. He'd gone over the matches obsessively for a while. He felt like he had some new killer tactics. But he also discovered that he had no desire to destroy Deep Blue, and that was something worth exploring. Slowly, Garry found himself easing off the chess pedal a little, working on his human rights campaigns, writing a book, enjoying his life and his now adult children. As Garry swiped through his iPhone, looking at pictures of him and Deep Blue at a winery in Southern California, a glass of cheeky zinfandel clutched awkwardly in the robot's claws, Garry might not always be happy, but he was content. Which is why the sudden development, the riposte was so unexpected and devastating.

Garry had been unhappy with the traditionalism and bureaucracy of the World Chess Federation for years. Surely, as he would continually say to Deep Blue, the media attention and success of their own match had demonstrated the public interest in chess. They just had to think outside the box. He didn't know when it was exactly, but at some point Deep Blue had inferred that Garry should create his own chess organisation — a rival one, with Garry at its head. He chewed on it for years, and then one day decided to take the plunge, in no small way supported by the knowledge his friend Deep Blue thought it was a good idea. When he went to the headquarters of the WCF to inform the head of his decision, he was polite but secretly jubilant. He could tell how much it irked them; the quiet grinding of teeth, the pained smiles. In the car on the way home, he stopped to buy a bottle of celebratory champagne and some of the expensive blue cheese that his robot friend liked. His phone rang, and it was the chair of the WCF, Ferdinand DeMarco.

'We wish you well in your exciting new endeavour,' the old fuck said blandly. 'Of course due to your … renunciation of our organisation, we will regrettably have to strip you of your World Champion status.'

'What … that's not fair!' protested Kasparov, shocked at how much the news hurt. He'd based his identity around this title for so long that it felt unnatural for it to be ripped away, and with so little ceremony. It wasn't even something he could fight for on the chessboard.

It was plain gone. He should have known they would retaliate.

'Wait, who is the new World Champion? Is it that weasel Anatoly?' he asked.
'Well, no ...' pondered DeMarco. 'Since Karpov has technically never defeated you. It would have to be ... why, Deep Blue of course.'

Garry Kasparov hung up the phone, fingers tingling with profound shock.

When he got home, he burst in through the front door. Early Madonna was playing on the speakers. He pushed through each room looking for Deep Blue. Finally, he found him in the master bedroom upstairs, in the middle of fucking Kasparov's adult son. A recording of Garry's voice started playing from Deep Blue.

'Chess is about the long game, about strategy,' spoke his voice, and Garry realised it was his speech from almost thirty years ago. It continued, mercilessly.

'I have devoted my life to this game. It's about knowing the best and truest way to destroy your opponent. What can a computer — even a super-computer — know about that?'

Garry swallowed nervously, struck at the patience, the inhuman, robotic savagery of Deep Blue's destruction of his life. Not only had the machine destroyed him in chess, but it had also played the long game, making moves so far ahead that Garry didn't even know he was still playing. He was ruined. No title, no career — and the thing that surprisingly tore into him like holy wounds, like blooms of stigmata in the dark, was the loss of his only friend. The recording stopped, the robot's eye flashing a dispassionate red. In a tinny robotic voice Deep Blue said:

'Check mate'.

HOME IS WHERE THE DAD IS

When Jason had left four years earlier, it had felt final, irrevocable. The huge steel and iron doors of his home had shut behind him with the airtight clang of destiny.

Perhaps it had been the drama that surrounded it: his father's wide sad face panicking the closer the elevator got to the surface and his weirdly soft hands pulling at his coat, at his packed bags, begging him to be careful, to be safe. The decision to leave home for university hadn't been easy. It had required a lot of willpower, a lot of careful arguments, a lot of soul-searching.

Jason genuinely believed he might never come back to his childhood home and had thought he was reconciled

to the idea. He truly felt like he had shed the cocoon
and now had to live his life outside its confinement,
hopefully as a butterfly, but potentially as some kind of
awful moth.

He remembered this glorious feeling of limitlessness
as he'd driven away, the endless vista of the horizon
stretching out in front of the highway, and the idea
of ever turning away from that expanse seemed
impossible.

But now he was back, all his belongings piled into the
back of his car, the same duffel he'd left with slung over
his shoulder. He'd thought he might have more things
to show for the four years he'd spent away, crafting a
life, but once he'd split all of his things with Damien, he
discovered it was mostly just clothes and books, and
one kinda funky chest of drawers he'd picked up when
they'd briefly thought they might become a couple who
buy antiques.

Jason sighed when he thought of Damien and sighed
again as he let the doors to his childhood home scan
his eyes and slowly open again to the outside world.

The elevator ride down into the bowels of the Earth
was as long as he remembered it; the various sprays
and mists and decontamination protocols as painful as
ever. But Jason was looking forward to coming home.
Obviously because he wanted to see his dad again, but
when he thought back on the past year — the terror of
finishing his degree, the horror of starting his first job,
and then the long agonising eight month breakup with

Damien — it all felt like chaos. He wanted to experience some stability again, some order.

Jason was looking forward to getting back into the slow rhythm of his youth: spending a day drying beans to put in jars, monitoring the various ebbs and flows of disease outbreak around the world, or really getting in there and giving the oxygen filters a thorough scrub. When you grew up in a hi-tech bunker buried in the Australian outback, designed by a man convinced the world would soon end from viral outbreak, there was ALWAYS something to do, a way to keep busy. It would be good for him, calming, relaxing. It would keep his mind off Damien.

'Son,' said his father, spreading his arms out wide, and enveloping him in a huge, if somewhat crinkly hug. Jason didn't take it personally that his only family had chosen to greet him in a full biohazard suit.
'It's so good to see you.'
'It's good to be back, dad,' said Jason, almost believing it as he said it.

There was a satisfying kind of melancholic drama about this whole thing. Perhaps everyone needs to go seventy feet underground to have their broken heart mended in a fully sterile environment?

'Good. Now let's go bathe you in bleach!' said his dad.

Dinner that night was equally as satisfying. His dad did a lot of nodding as Jason got wine drunk and expounded on where things went wrong with Damien.

Every so often he'd break in with a bit of homespun wisdom, which Jason enjoyed, and felt was probably good advice, but that he forgot almost immediately. He could get the gist: be patient, believe in himself, move to a small Canadian island to raise greyhounds. That last one was actually something Jason had been considering and was a weird career change his father had only slightly raised his eyebrows at.

But all the energy, all that frantic pain and the spur it provided faded away in the morning, when Jason would be awoken early in the unrelenting darkness of his windowless room by the loud hiss of the air recycling unit, missing the warmth of Damien's thick arms wrapped around him, his breath softer and gentler on the back of his neck.

Jason also felt something was off about the way his heartbreak-recovery narrative was playing out. Sure, there were jobs to do — a bunker didn't run itself after all — but his father seemed a distracted, slightly disinterested presence in the whole thing.

'Just swept out the monoxide filter,' he grunted to his dad after a gruelling three hours of work.
'Oh, right, good, yeah,' his dad answered, looking startled while rifling through a drawer.
'What are you looking for?' asked Jason, feeling more than a little deflated.
'Oh, um ... shirt.'

Things only got weirder when that night he saw his dad disappear into his room, wearing the so-called shirt, a

colourful (if faded) button-up affair dating back to the
seventies that sent out a loud reek of mothballs.

'There's egg powder on the bench if you want dinner,
son,' he called over his shoulder before slamming the
door shut.
Jason sighed and began making egg.

As the week dragged on, Jason began to suspect his
dad had something going on, something outside his
usual obsessive interest in smallpox statistics. Every
night he'd disappear into his room, and the light
would stay on for hours. Meanwhile, Jason wasn't
finding counting the legume stores as soothing as
he predicted. It mostly made him think about what
Damien was up to: the parties he was going to, the
fun he was having, the boys he was meeting. When
Jason met Damien, he'd been drawn in by his laugh
— it was loud and boundless and had clearly never
been confined, stifled, by close metal walls, layers of
lead, and leagues of dank, muffled earth. He hated
to think how more moths would be drawn into the
sunshine of that laugh now that he was gone. Jason let
the chickpeas trickle through his hands like protein
packed missed opportunities.

One night, after his dad slammed the door again,
this time wearing a tuxedo jacket of all things, Jason
slammed a bottle of red wine (his dad was keen on
red wine, it helped fight off radioactive poisoning
apparently) and decided that he needed some more
wisdom because he was sad. So, he gave a perfunctory
knock and entered his dad's room.

Jason didn't know what he expected to see, but he'd never expected to interrupt his famously reclusive, apocalypse-prepper father on a date. Glowing from the computer monitor in a Zoom window was a grey-haired lady with huge glasses who was smiling fondly at his dad. There was a half-drunk glass of wine resting near the keyboard and his dad was smiling and gesticulating and flushed with pleasure.

'Oh, ah, Jason — this is Mirabelle. Belle, this is my son Jason. I told you he was visiting.'
Her voice came through the speakers, tinny and with a deep southern accent.
'Jason, it's a real pleasure.'
Jason would later find out that she lived in a bunker somewhere in the Arizona desert, and the two had met on an online forum where people who were really scared of global viruses would go to trade tips and hints.

'Is there something I can do for you buddy?' said Jason's dad, eyes flickering back towards his wizened online girlfriend.
 Something about the whole situation tipped Jason over the edge. His eyes filled with hot tears and he shrugged.
'I'm ... sad. Sad.'
Jason's dad stood up and patted him a few times on the shoulder.
'Son, I say this with love, but you just gotta remember: no matter how sad it is, how bad you feel, it's not the end of the world. Trust me, I would know.'

A LETTER FROM A DYING SOLDIER TO HIS SWEETHEART WHO HE HAD NEVER FULFILLED SEXUALLY

The soldier bled onto the snow like a slushie machine gone wrong, gone damn bad, crimson blooming onto the pristine icy whiteness.

'Captain,' the man sobbed, curled around his broken guts. 'Am I gonna be alright?'
'Sure, Marchenko,' crooned Captain Jack Manning of the US Army, cradling the soldier's head in his gloved hands. 'You're gonna be fine little buddy.'

He peered over the man's head at the last remaining medic in the company, who shook his head sadly, and then made a face and shrugged his shoulders.

'We'll get that patched up and you'll be poppin' Russki

skulls with that pea-shooter in no time — or you'll be trying,' Manning joshed, his eyes sad.

'Never was a good shot,' Marchenko admitted. 'Maybe if I had been ... I'd have nailed the bastard before he got me.'

'If wishes were fishes, we'd all have mercury poisoning,' said Jack.

There was the sound of gunfire in the distance that carried across the snow like a handful of stones falling on ice. Captain Jack jerked his head at two of the men near to him, who checked their rifles and trudged out of the shadow of the ice-cliff they were huddled behind, into the swirling snowstorm.

'Captain,' gasped Marchenko. 'I need you to ... promise me something.'

'Hey, none of that talk now, private,' shushed Jack, looking pained.

'No — listen to me!' Marchenko wheezed, using what little strength he had left to grasp the Captain's arm with his bloodstained hands.

'My wife, Dolores ... back in Ohio ... please give her this letter I wrote ... it's nothing much ... just three pages of me describing what army pants feel like ... I'm pretty emotionally repressed ...'

'It's a generational thing,' said Jack, soothingly.

He fumbled at his breast pocket, pulling from it a faded polaroid of a pretty young lady with close-set eyes and elaborate curls.

'Geez, Marchenko, she's gorgeous! You dog!' kidded Jack.

'Yeah, she's a pearl,' he croaked. 'We only been married for half a year before I shipped out ... now she's a widow ... and I never got her that baby she wanted.'
'C'mon, Marchenko,' protested Jack.

Marchenko's body shuddered and his liver popped out of the gaping hole that used to be his torso.

'Promise me, Captain ... promise me ...'
'Anything, Marchenko. You don't need to worry, I'll do anything,' said the Captain, grabbing the man's slippery hand with his own.
'Marry ... my wife ... and give her the child she always wanted. You're the only man who deserves her ...' the dying man wheezed.
'Ah, geez,' said the Captain.
'Promise me ... and ... and make sure you pleasure her physically ... because I never properly learned ...'
'Ah, geeeeeez,' repeated the Captain.
'I need you to ... impregnate my wife, Captain ... promise me ...'
'I guess?'
'I was a selfish lover,' said Marchenko, his last breath rattling from his lips as the blood stopped pumping from his heart and all over himself.
'Goddamn,' muttered Jack, looking down at the young man's blank features, which were already covered in a thin layer of frost. 'And goddamn this war.'

BEACH BODIES

H illary didn't know exactly why she maintained her friendship with her old circle from high school.

It's not like they were bad people, and their annual dinner together was hardly an onerous use of time, it's just that Martha, Sally, Stacey and Stacy were ... well, basic. Not that Hillary was particularly edgy herself these days, but travelling back to the suburbs to see them really did heighten the difference between their lives. They talked about their children, they complained about their husbands, they gossiped about the neighbourhood. They were basic. Hillary had a good career and a fresh, remarkably enjoyable divorce, and a subscription to TWO theatres, which she often thought about going to. It was sometimes hard to relate.

But as they sat around Stacey's newly renovated dining room (which they'd discussed for almost an hour) Hillary was forcefully reminded of exactly why she left these dinners feeling so flat and insecure and sad: it was beach body season.

'I cannot WAIT for winter to be over,' purred Martha over her glass of sauvignon blanc (that she'd picked up from a darling winery).

Hillary tensed, knowing what was coming next.

'Time to start working on our beach bodies!' chuckled Sally, who laughed a lot but never said anything funny.

Hillary rolled her eyes behind her rosé. Honestly, every year they talked about their beach bodies and every year they stayed exactly the same. Wouldn't it be better to just give up instead of constantly flagellating themselves (and others) by talking about it?

'You should join us, Hillary! Get yourself a beach body for the new year.'

Instead of politely shutting the ridiculous idea down like she did every year, Hillary had suddenly had enough. Maybe she would join them and actually find out what the hell they did each year. Maybe she'd help whip them into shape. Hell, maybe she'd get fitter and happier herself. Maybe she'd find some widower dad

and fuck him. She didn't give a shit about a beach
body (who goes to the beach?) but she wouldn't mind
getting slightly hotter. Fuck it, thought Hillary, maybe
this year I'll be basic too?

'That sounds lovely,' she said, and immediately felt
strangely good about herself.

A few days later, she stood on a cold beach in the early
hours of the morning in her bathers, arms futilely
crossed over her goose-pimpled body, trying to
protect herself from the cold wind.

She watched in numb confusion, in freezing
bemusement, as her oldest friends splashed into
the icy blue ocean and lay in the shallows, splayed
and limp. Tumbled by the waves into the sand,
the cold turning their skin marbled alabaster and
blue, crumbed in sand and adorned with wreaths of
seaweed.

Martha floated facedown in the ocean, slowly pulled
away from land by a rip. Sally lay chuckling and bloated
in the shallows with a crab crawling through her hair
while Stacey and Stacy were pulled back and forth
by the waves, flopping like shipwreck victims, like
corpses, while gulls wheeled overhead.

CONTROL VARIABLE

The lizards were not sick but they were not well. Despite their lack of any identifiable wounds or parasites or infections, they were twisted little things, pale and lethargic and mostly disinterested in each other. They slumped in their expensive habitat, occasionally scratching at bits of their skin. Brenda ground her teeth in frustration as she stared into their huge, luxurious tank. Its state-of-the-art UV heat lamp throbbed merrily in the corner like a miniature sun, reflecting off painfully crafted brackish ponds and highlighting rare cultured ferns. The tank was — scientifically — as perfect as possible. Yet even as she dumped in some carefully caught and nutritionally optimal flying bugs, the lizards only blinked apathetically. She knew from experience that the lizards would wait for the insects to slow down and eventually die before they would sadly pick at their corpses.

'Tea, Brenda?' intoned a rich voice from the next lab that slid down Brenda's spine like warm molasses. Brenda looked down at her mug full of cold liquid, noting that she'd been too distracted to remove the crumpled tea bag which had leaked flecks of leaf into her mug.

'I'm FINE,' called back Brenda in what she hoped passed for a polite tone. 'Thanks,' she added begrudgingly.

'No problem at all,' came back the voice. Brenda waited until she heard the door out of the adjoining lab slam close and footsteps disappear towards the kitchen area before she screamed into her hand. Once she was done, she stalked into the next-door lab, white coat flapping behind her like a wizard's cape in a furious tempest. This lab was identical in design to her own: the same fluorescent lights, the same racks of scientific paraphernalia. Yet, Brenda knew there was one glaring difference. She put her face against the lizard enclosure in this lab and breathed a plume of frustrated air against the glass. Inside the tank, under the bright lights of their own UV ray, around the same configuration of ponds and lichen-encrusted rocks, the lizards ... frolicked. There was no other word for it. The way the tiny, thumbnail-sized creatures swam or sun baked, or chased each other through a labyrinth of tunnels and ferns was distinctly playful.

The scientific part of her brain dispassionately noted the signs of good health and the clutches of eggs that outnumbered her own brood's efforts substantially. The other part of her brain, the non-scientist part, made her squish her face even further against the glass, and hiss 'fuuuuuuuuuuck yoooooooooouuuuuu' to the happy lizards.

Deirdre kicked open the door to the lab, balancing a steaming mug in one hand and a haphazard sheaf of notes in the other. She was humming loudly, although it trailed off as she noticed Brenda peering into her lizard tank.

'Oh, hello,' Deidre said.

Brenda grunted before realising she wasn't being shouted at through a closed door, and social conventions meant she should probably justify being in her colleague's lab. Brenda would hate it if Deirdre came into her space while she was out.

'Umm,' said Brenda cleverly. 'Can I borrow ... this?' She picked up a random beaker.

Deirdre nodded, bemused. Deirdre was one of those people that mightn't be classically beautiful, but always seemed lit by an inner glow that made her stunning. Or perhaps she was just flushed, thought Brenda sourly, forcing herself to stop admiring the woman's soft lips and kind eyes.

'Are you ok Brenda?' Deidre asked sincerely, seeking

eye contact. 'I know it's been a bit of a time for you lately, if you know what I mean.'

She truly did know what Deidre meant. Despite all of Brenda's work, the late hours, the rigorous application of scientific principles and lab practicalities and good old fashioned elbow grease, Brenda's work was not doing well. As a scientist, she'd grown accustomed to failure as a learning concept, but there were also rumbles that funding was becoming ... sparse. She had been warned that without some presentable results to the board, her experiments may lose financial support — especially when her results were compared to Deidre's glowing and, most importantly, bankable lizards.

Deirdre reached out a hand and rubbed Brenda's shoulder. There had been a time when Deirdre and Brenda had been extremely good friends. They had even gotten margaritas at a bar once after teaching a lecture hall full of snotty undergrads. It had been the perfect night.

Brenda pulled her arm away, clutching the beaker to her chest. 'I'm fine,' she muttered, scurrying back into her lab and slamming the door.

Later, long after Deirdre had gone home, or more likely to a bar with her beautiful friends, Brenda noticed something new in the lizard tank. Noting the time, she used her instruments to zoom in and saw with a sinking sensation that one of her subjects was covered entirely in a sheath of fungus, slowly dragging

its spindly body across the sand. She wasn't sure
where it was trying to get to, but before too long it
was exhausted, lying still, barely breathing. Brenda
tried to control her own breathing, a technique she'd
learned from a yoga class she attended with Deirdre
many years ago. She dragged in a gasp of hard, cold
air, and then expelled it in a scream. The fungus wasn't
a death sentence for her lizards. She knew exactly
the fungicide needed. But it was a death sentence for
her project; there was no way she could expect to be
funded again after this. She picked up a metal tray
and threw it across the room, taking obscure delight
in the loudness of the clatter in the normally peaceful
environment. She followed it up with a jar of pipettes,
which rained down on the room in shards. It was
also satisfying. She picked up a beaker, aiming it at
her dusty framed PhD hung up behind her desk, but
stopped at the last moment. She looked at the beaker,
her rage transmuted from hot and unfocused into
something cold and defined. *Interesting*, she thought.
Worth exploring further.

It only took a month before Deirdre left her lab
entirely, leaving behind some good-natured sighs,
a lot of aspirational quotes like 'when god closes
a door, he opens a window' and 'on to bigger and
better things' and 'change is better than a holiday'.
The faculty had been regretful about cutting off her
funding, but unfortunately in this current financial
climate, continuing an unsatisfactory experiment
with a specimen lot infected by fungus was simply
unsustainable. Brenda was surprised at how little
remorse she felt. She expected to be wracked by

guilt after methodically switching her sick lizards with Deirdre's peppy, healthy ones in a manner so gradual and slow, she would never suspect a thing. She expected to feel like a bad person. But, if there was one thing that Brenda understood, it was efficiency. She barely even needed to justify to herself that ultimately it was for science, rather than personal gain. She'd always been good at achieving her goals and now she felt like nothing would stand in her way ever again. Brenda looked forward to a bountiful future of healthy lizards and uncontested lizard grants.

However, it wasn't long before Brenda realised there was something wrong with her new aspirational life path. For one thing, the lizards soon lost their perk. They stopped frolicking, and instead possessed an attitude of ... anticipation. They spent a lot of time still, patient and waiting. Brenda decided that it was simply the same winter chill that had settled in her bones since the seasons changed, and she upped the temperature by a few degrees. But it didn't help and before her despairing eyes, she watched as Deirdre's formerly golden lizards morphed into the misshapen albino horrors from her previous tank. It made no sense. There was literally no reason for this to happen, no deviation from the way Deirdre had cared for the lizards. The only difference was Brenda looked after them. It was as if she was cursed, a truth she refused to accept. It was not scientifically sound thinking.

If Brenda had looked herself in the mirror for longer than a few cursory moments each morning — and sometimes not even then, as she'd taken to spending

nights in her lab, watching the lizards feverishly,
completely mirrorless — she'd have noticed an
interesting similarity between her and the creatures.
She, too, grew pale and sickly, stunted and bent
beneath the weight of her large head. Her eyes seemed
to grow in protuberance, and her fingers, once so deft
and agile in the manipulation of microscopes and
Bunsen burners, curled like claws. She let her food
grow cold and congealed, picking at it in a desultory
manner. Brenda, like her lizards, was not doing well.
And late one night, the ruins of a day-old fish spread
out in front of her for dinner, surrounded by notes and
graphs and spreadsheets, Brenda pinpointed what had
changed for her lizards.

Deirdre was sleepy and mussed when she answered the
door to her apartment, looking casually devastating in
a linen robe, but still ushered Brenda in out of the cold,
putting the kettle on.

'This is an unexpected pleasure,' Deirdre chuckled,
pulling mugs out of her cupboard.

Brenda had no time for small talk. She scuttled closer
to Deirdre, looking up at the taller woman with fierce,
searching eyes.

'What is it?' she asked.
'What's what, Brenda? What's going on?' answered
Deirdre, clearly concerned now.
'You were giving the lizards something extra,
something special. YOU are the control variable I
hadn't accounted for. You are the reason your lizards

do better. What is it? Vitamins? Steroids?'
'Your lizards ended up doing better than mine,'
laughed Deirdre, ruefully.

Brenda hissed, frustrated by her inability to either
get the answers she needed or talk about her own
sabotage.

'The science doesn't make sense!' Brenda continued,
grabbing Deirdre with her strong fingers.
'Not everything is about science,' answered Deirdre,
defensively. 'Sometimes, lizards just need a little love.'
Deirdre pointed to a tank in her apartment's living
room in which a score of Brenda's former fungus-
ridden lizards cavorted happily, neon green and
beaming with vitality.
'Impossible,' whispered Brenda, running a clammy
hand down the side of the glass. The lizards inside
scattered, disappearing into holes in the ground.
'Although ... no, it makes sense.'

Brenda knew the evidence was incontrovertible: it
was indeed Deirdre's love that marked the difference
between lacklustre lizards and happy lizards. She
had enough test subjects to prove this conclusively.
She even thought back to herself — how she had tried
to disappear into her work after leaning across her
margarita to kiss Deirdre, only to have her apologise
and pull away. How she had grown darker and more
harrowed after she betrayed Deirdre, starved for even
those remaining few gestures of love. She wondered,
idly, if she could measure the potency of love from
Deirdre that she had relied upon in those gestures —

the cups of tea, the odd statement of support.

'Could the missing link be ... love?' spat Brenda, mind
working furiously, back hunched, and grimy hair falling
in greased ringlets over her eyes. 'No, that's insane!
Insane! Unless?'
'I think it's time you left now,' suggested Deirdre from
the kitchen, hesitantly and with the same gentle pity
she'd shown after she'd pulled back from Brenda's
attempted kiss in that bar.

The lizards were doing so much better, and Brenda
took a lot of glee in reporting it in her notes. They
didn't frolic anymore, but they were robust and
healthy. They had recently started competing for
territory, driving weaker lizards away from the prime
sunny rocks near the food chutes. Some of them had
gone scarlet and a deep rusty red. Once again Brenda
thought she'd feel worse than she did, but with such
magnificent results it was hard to linger on any feelings
of horror. It was simply a shame she could never
properly release the scientific findings from her new
'love-based diet' for the lizards. It wasn't fear for her
own wellbeing — she always put science first after all
— but if she went to gaol, the lizards would soon suffer.
She pressed a button labelled 'love' and with a noise
like an old ice dispenser, chunks of raw bloody meat
were dispensed from a tube into the lizard tank. The
lizards went wild, swarming in a feeding frenzy, their
healthy bodies glistening with vigour and strength.
Love truly was the best medicine.

UNTOLD TALES OF KINDNESS AND CHARITY

Jeremy struggled beneath the weight of the novelty sized cheque, sweating uncomfortably, feeling it slip through his greasy fingers, like he was actually trying to hold on to twenty thousand dollars worth of gold coins, rather than simply a bigger than normal slab of cardboard. The mayor stood next to him, smiling so relentlessly that her teeth looked hard and dry. The photographer from the paper kept snapping photos and saying things like 'alright, just one more, looking cool bananas, that's great, here we go!'

The cheque slipped again, and he wondered if it was trying to flee from his hands and go to someone who had actually earned it.

Jeremy had been featured once before in the local newspaper, many years ago as a tiny goblin-faced soccer youth who'd broken his leg so badly on the field that they had to send a helicopter from the city to fly him to the hospital. There was still a curling, yellowed copy of that edition of the *Balgowlah Leader* in his dad's study, the front page showcasing Jeremy and his massive leg cast, giving a thumbs up to the camera, surrounded by ads for discount meat at the butcher. It had been a uniquely thrilling form of fame for a child, which had given him notoriety in the town, his shattered femur somehow managing to boost him above his formless, anonymous peers in the eyes of the locals.

In this town, children were like those crab migrations you'd get on a tropical island: swarming in huge numbers, often irritating, extremely hungry, but one day you wake up and they're gone, naturally scuttled off to study at big-city TAFEs, to audition for *The Voice*, to marry short but successful tennis players, never to return. It was pretty rare to stand out as a kid in Balgowlah. Jeremy of course, had returned, slinking back into town after his big-city restaurant went bust, getting a job at one of the three local pubs (admittedly the best one), watching *Million Dollar Hot Seat* with his silent dad and going back to sleep in his childhood bedroom.

Jeremy had never expected to be back on the front page of the *Leader*, especially not twenty years later, his mischievous little gremlin features replaced by eye-bags and wrinkles. He hadn't even had to break his other leg to do it this time. Jeremy realised why he felt so guilty as the photographer took snap after snap of him and five other people standing in front of Mrs McGowan's old house, holding her little black book between them, giving the thumbs up, giant novelty cheques being handed to them by the mayor.

Shattering his leg bones so badly that doctors had to fill him up with metal pins and glue was something worth noting, was something he hadn't sought out, but through virtue of suffering he'd deserved that attention. It might have happened to him accidentally; a collision with both destiny and a boy named Bryce who was built like a prepubescent stack of Christmas hams. But you could never argue it wasn't Jeremy's leg that had snapped like kindling, or Jeremy's rat-face, which flew above them all on a helicopter.

'She came in once a week for a loaf of bread and some finger buns,' enthused a teen nearby, who unconsciously counted on her fingers as she spoke to the reporter. 'Once she bought a vanilla slice, but I watched her take one bite of it and throw it away once she left the store. I guess she was trying something new, I don't know.'

The reporter blinked and scratched on his pad. Jeremy saw he'd written 'vanilla slice?' with a huge question mark.

'But like, I'll be honest, it's not like we spoke, like it's not that she was mean to me, she was just polite, didn't really say anything, except for her order ...'

The girl paused, and then visibly brightened. 'Although there was one thing … like a year ago, it was raining and she must have slipped a bit when she walked out of the store, and I watched her drop the finger buns. And you know, she was old, so I felt kinda sorry for her … and don't tell my boss, this is off the record or whatever, but I just grabbed some more buns and gave them to her, it was like four dollars. I guess that could be it?'

The reporter shook his head in disbelief, wrote 'finger buns' and then circled it dramatically.

It had been like this all day — people breathlessly questioning the six of them, trying to work out why each of them had been gifted twenty thousand dollars from the town's wealthiest, most reclusive, most famously hostile resident. According to the only solicitor in Balgowlah, she had specified before she died that every name she'd written in her little black notebook, which she kept on her person at all times, was to be given some of her money on the first day of the new year. Unfortunately, she had died before this date came around, making the planned act of kindness accidentally posthumous. Jeremy had seen his own name written in the book in scratchy old lady writing, in ink like squid blood.

And that's how the mystery unravelled, with all the people written in the black book suddenly remembering small, untold tales of kindness and charity they'd committed near the widow McGowan, which they'd mostly forgotten about. But this old woman — who for years had her huge and lonely house

egged every Halloween, who was known only by the
cardinal sins of being rich and private — had noticed,
and she'd written it all down. There was the plumber
who, as a gangly teenager on the way to school, noticed
Mrs McGowan's huge hissing cat stuck in a eucalyptus
tree and had taken it upon himself to climb up in his
little school shorts and rescue it, delivering the yowling
mass of fur and leaves back to the house. There was
the neighbour on her left, a pragmatic single mum
named Bernice, whose relentless campaign to fend
the bins on the street against the rampaging crows,
had not gone unnoticed. A boy from Jeremy's year in
high school vaguely remembered carrying home a split
plastic bag of tomatoes for an old woman once who
he'd noticed wearing an outrageous number of pearls.

When asked, Jeremy felt thick greasy sweat start to
drip down his forehead and in a panic he shrugged and
said 'oh you know, just helped out a bit'. Luckily, he was
mostly ignored as reporters were lured away by the
comparative glamour of the dropped finger buns story.
But Jeremy was not just being coy, or modest as the
mayor implied while firmly shaking his hand in front of
a camera, Jeremy was actually one hundred percent
sure he'd never done a kind thing for Mrs McGowan.

Looking back through his memories, frantically,
systematically, Jeremy was sure he didn't deserve
this money because he'd never done anything kind
for anyone. Sure, he'd done things like help his friend
move house and donate to the odd charity. He'd
never been cruel. He served people beers at work, he
watched old video tapes of *Terminator 2: Judgement*

Day with his dad, gone for a swim in the morning. He'd certainly never done anything kind for Mrs McGowan. In fact, he was reasonably sure he'd never met her. Just knew of her, like a legend, like a ghost, like a famous second cousin.

Now, he felt judged by the ghost of the town's most unapproachable widow.

Later that day, once the reporters had fled back to their water-damaged offices, once the mayor had folded herself into her hatchback and driven to the beach to present awards to tiny shivering nippers, Jeremy found himself wandering through the grounds of Mrs McGowan's now empty manor, as he considered the newfound knowledge that he was selfish. He asked himself: what was the point of his life? What did he bring to the world?

Amongst all the pruned hedges and gently twinkling ponds, he ran into his dad, mowing the lawn. It wasn't too surprising, that was what his dad did for a living, mowed lawn, but Jeremy had never known he'd worked here on the McGowan property. Turns out he actually knew next to nothing about his dad. What he did with his days, who he drank with at the bowling club, what kind of man he was. Would a critical millionaire widow have looked at his dad and seen a good man? Probably. Now that he thought of it, he could recall a dozen small moments of graciousness he'd seen his dad commit: the way he always humoured the verbose old timers at the pub with a patient ear, the way he'd good naturedly clutched at his chest and fallen into a pile of leaves the other day when a neighbourhood kid pretended to shoot him with a water pistol, the way he'd pop around to help out dozens of his clients deal with possum issues outside of hours.

Now that he thought about it, Jeremy had to wonder at the fallibility of Mrs McGowan; had she even known the right member of the family to give the money to? Had she been watching his dad trimming her shrubbery, thinking it was Jeremy? Maybe all men looked young, indistinct, to someone as old as Mrs McGowan. Perhaps Jeremy's fame as the boy who broke his leg so badly a helicopter came and took him away had eclipsed his humble, quiet dad?

Jeremy suddenly felt the giddy wave of a decision sweep over him; he was about to make his first selfless act, his first little story of kindness. He could almost feel the ghost of the widow McGowan smile benevolently upon him, her permed grey hair stiff and buoyant with approval.

'Dad!' he called out, jogging over. 'I've got good news, you're going on holidays!'

It wasn't huge in the scheme of things, to use most of his money to send his dad overseas. But it was kind — his dad sometimes watched travel shows and said things like 'gee whiz' and 'imagine that' in incredulous tones when he saw big waterfalls or old buildings. He'd never travelled farther than Queensland, never really taken a break beyond a couple of weeks at Christmas, usually in a caravan park down the coast. So, in that sense it was maybe the first time Jeremy had thought of a specific way to be kind to him. And he was rewarded with a series of terribly angled photos, blurry and shadowed, of his dad sunburnt and awkward and happy outside of the Taj Mahal, lying on a tropical beach, pointing at a huge bird eating a mango. It was nice, and it didn't get in the paper, but he was glad he did it.

Many, many years later, after Jeremy's dad died of old age and a bad heart, he found hidden in his study almost fifteen years of correspondence between his dad and Mrs McGowan: a long, romantic, often uncomfortably erotic relationship they'd kept secret, between a very old woman and her younger paramour. That was shock enough, but it also helped finally explain why he'd been given the money.

'Good lord Frank, do I have to give that boy money to get him out of your house? He could go open his little restaurant up again,' she wrote, her letters like a malicious crab scuttling across the page. 'He's cramping our style and I'm too old to put up with suspicious adult children. Hide your sad boy. He won't have to know a thing. I'll just make it look like I'm giving money to a whole bunch of people in town, for being good citizens or what have you. I haven't seen you for days, I miss you. I love you Frank and I'm very rich and impatient and I always get what I want. And I want you.'

THE DOG PARK

Bono had shut down America. He had uploaded his face into every computer, every internet fridge, his thick layer of face-skin stretched and held intact only by his trademark glasses. Bono looking at you from your microwave, listening while you talked to the doctor, winking at you from your original Gameboy. Nothing was cool anymore. I was at the dog park when I heard they were bringing back Princess Diana to try and stop it all, a horrible computer version of her to do battle with Bono in the veins of fibre optic cables running beneath the ocean.

I go to the dog park because my Staffy, Prue, needs to run at least twice a day or she gets a crazed look in her eyes and disappears into my spare room and I become too scared to find out what she's done in there.

'There's that delicious bitch, Prue,' the other dog owners will mutter, as we arrive, pulling out their own leads in preparation to leave. It's not that Prue is a violent dog, not like Sapphire, the tooth bristling Maltese Terrier who bites at the inside of dogs' cheeks and makes big hounds slink to the boundaries of the fence upon seeing her. Prue has a big gap-toothed maw and a pink tongue like a bathmat. She is a brown barrel of affection. She loves to get a human to put their whole fist in her mouth. That is how much she wants to be close to you.

But she also loves other dogs and other dogs love her. They think she is magic. They think she is delicious. When Prue runs, her stumpy legs and bread loaf body barrelling along with the other dogs, she eventually vomits in an effort to keep up. A simple dumping of her stomach's entire contents in one efficient gag. When this happens, the other dogs go wild because they think what Prue has in her stomach is magic dog food and they can't resist. The other dog owners hate seeing their puppies eat a big pile of Prue's vomit.

Prue came to me almost a year ago. I found her in my house one day, a tiny puppy with a pink bow around her neck, sitting in a spreading puddle of urine. A note said:

Your life sickens me, do something useful for god's sake, here's a dog.

Dr. Sarah Mont Blanc

Dr. Mont Blanc was the counsellor that the Duty Free store I worked at hired to help treat my trauma. I'd never been to a shrink before. I tried to remember stories about my mother. She grew up in a factory and at home would make thirty sandwiches at the start of each month in a long assembly line, teaching me to eat all the fish and chicken sandwiches first, so I could avoid food poisoning, or at least lessen it. I prepared these stories of my mother thinking I'd have to lie on a leather couch and recount them, but Dr. Mont Blanc never asked for them. Instead, she would take me for long drives in her car, berating me in a steady Swedish monotone.

Apart from the fact they resent my dog and her edible bile, the other people at the park are wary. They are alternately standoffish or the kind of pleasant that raises the voice an entire octave, like a queen condescending to talk to the small child that burns her sheets every morning. The other dog owners can tell I was in the Black Tuesday Sale Riots. I have all the tell-tale scars. Long gouges from fingernails down my face, a dent in my skull from a thrown cash register, intermittent coupon shakes, barcode myopia, Eftpos burns. Instead of making them uncomfortable, I sit under the furthest tree with an old man who never seems to leave the park. His dog, an ancient Westie, looks upon the frantic efforts of his peers with tired, disdainful eyes. The old man's name is Jeremiah, and he is excellent company because he only grunts hello and goodbye, and says, 'there's the shark, heh heh heh' when he sees Prue.

Jeremiah was watching the prancing star of the park, a Fox Terrier by the name of Mack. Mack is cute as all hell, and you can't help but love him. Love him and hate him at the same time, like cyanide donuts, or the digital spectre of Princess Diana (who is our only hope). Jeremiah watched as Mack jumped into his owner's arms in a spontaneous outburst of affection, and he turned to me and said, 'There was a fella just like that one on my last ship. Boy that kid could dance, dance and sing and make a compass point north just by wailing at it. Never seen his like on the ocean before and not since. Of course he didn't last long — not for long. Not for long.'

I couldn't tell if he was laughing or crying. Jeremiah was covered in scars from the time he was swallowed by a whale. This made me feel comfortable with him, more at ease with my tinnitus, which was the beeping sound of a barcode scanner, echoing sonorously in the distance of my head.

During the Black Tuesday Riots, when fear of Cyber-Bono spreading into our airlines meant that Duty Free would be shut down for good, people went mad trying to buy cheap booze and perfumes and electronic goods. Thousands perished. I'd watched in frozen horror as a woman tried to carry seventy-three bottles of Johnny Walker Red Label. Her spine slowly bent backwards under the weight until it snapped with the sound of a hard shoe stepping on a soft biscuit. My diet is now soups and mashes, anything without a crackle. I also have a strong aversion to people with prominent spines, but I feel like it's something I'm working through.

I was reluctant to tell Dr. Mont Blanc about Jeremiah and his troubling sea-stories. I don't really socialise with anybody anymore and the subject of her rants is often concerned with 'how much of a fucking annoying dick you are because you don't make jokes or talk about relevant life experiences which relate to something that someone else is talking about, oh my god'. In order to combat this, she drove me to a party one night against my wishes. It was a seventies-style key party, and she yelled to the room, 'Just ignore this guy, he's just here to watch,' and then told her husband to 'dream a little bigger this time, don't go for the obvious keys, fuck you're making me look bad'. She was annoyed but understanding when someone snapped a cracker while going for an unrealistic amount of salsa.

'I should have realised this dump would have crackers,' she snarled.

At the park a woman with two obnoxiously white Malamutes wished me a good morning. I ignored her spine, the flimsy bone-hose that kept her politely smiling face wobbling on top of her feet. I wished her a good morning back. After a few moments of silence, she tentatively touched my arm, which had been shattered in two places by huge bulk bottles of Ralph Lauren perfume.

'I just wanted to say thank you for what you did on Black Tuesday, you're a hero.'

I shook my head. Not because I'm modest but because while all this was happening, while fathers knifed their own children for nougat, while mothers called lightning from the sky for more shopping trolleys, all I did was stay at my register, mindlessly scanning. The real heroes were on computer terminals, listening to U2 songs until their ears bled, trying to find a way to halt the inevitable Bono flood.

'Do you think our Unholy Princess Diana will bring back the Duty Free?' asked the woman hopefully.

'Yes,' I whispered, blinking back tears.

Prue vomited at my feet, and the other dogs piled in, ruthless and desperate and thrilled.

EGG

The call came through at 2am. It was one of the agents in Berlin. I whispered 'hello' even though I could tell Brian had been awoken by my ringtone. He exhaled slow and annoyed.

'Boss,' said the voice through the phone, piercing in the cold silence of the night. 'Boss, we found one.'

I muffled a gasp, flushed by triumph, panicking in silence.

'Egg?' murmured Brian next to me, sitting up slightly and disturbing Christina, our labrador who slept under the blankets near our feet.

'We found one,' I said softly, the words catching in my throat.

★ ★ ★

I'm talking to a diplomat, an ambassador from a European country. Brian looks better than me in a tuxedo and is asking the ambassador lots of earnest and thoughtful questions about his home country. The ambassador is telling us about how the bridges are old and beautiful and how there are catacombs underneath them, full of secrets. The ambassador finishes describing an old brass statue and asks me what I do for a living. Who am I to be eating canapes in this marble building?

'He works for the UN,' says Brian, rubbing the small of my back.
'Ah,' says the ambassador, raising his eyebrows.
'I head a research team,' I say uncomfortably, feeling the bowtie constricting my throat. 'We're looking into the business with the toasters. We've been working for … years now. Years.'
'Ah yes, very curious,' says the ambassador, looking over my shoulder. 'You must excuse me. I see a small bowl of olives.'

I was used to this sort of reaction ever since the world woke to discover not a single toaster worked anymore. There'd been a brief panic; a few months of science articles and conversations on TV. The UN had put together my team of forty investigators and scientists

and agents tasked with getting to the bottom of this
… anomaly. This global breaking down of an everyday
appliance. But as the world spun on, as the looming
reality of rising sea levels and elections and the return
of the mammoths took over the news cycle, people
forgot about the toasters. People learned to grill their
bread or use toasted sandwich makers. It became a
curiosity, an embarrassment. They wanted to forget
ever having toasters.

In the lab I pointed out the toaster to an impatient
six-star general. It was red with decades of crumbs
crusted around its classic two-slit structure. It had
been bought from a bewildered grandma for over two
million dollars.

'So what makes this one so special? Why does it work
and none of the others?' he barks.

I shrug. As far as we can tell it's just a toaster.

'Some things just work,' I said, thinking of Brian and
how young and handsome and interesting he is and
how I'm merely a toaster researcher nicknamed Egg.
Thinking of our hot crowded bed on a cold night.
Thinking of how the mammoths got cloned and
everyone loved them.

FAREWELL, STARS *HOLLOW*

They shot Kirk first. Maybe it was the US Marshalls or maybe it was the fire department. I don't know. There's a lot I don't remember from those times, a lot of blurry memories. A lot of things I try not to remember to be honest. They put all of Stars Hollow under martial law to evacuate us from the wildfire rushing towards us, loading us all into yellow school buses, throwing our suitcases onto the ground, pulling a crying, wild-eyed Babette away from her cat. They didn't have time for Kirk, who arrived in his own high-vis vest, with clipboard and megaphone, shouting contradictory orders.

'Taylor designated me as town crisis management,' he said while the dense wall of black smoke and hellish red

clouds galloped closer to us every second.
'I've developed my own system,' he said. It was very
eccentric, naturally.

When he held up the buses for over five minutes, they
shot him in the head. There wasn't time to indulge in
the town's various weirdos and wackos. Not this time.
Later on they shot Taylor, too, and some of the other
townspeople whose names I had never learned, who
drifted through my early life in the background, like
extras in a sitcom. They shot them too. The last time I
saw Stars Hollow was through the blurry back window
of a bus and the sulphuric light from the fire and the
drifting snowfall of ash made it look like an old sepia
photo, a thing from the past, a distant memory.

'I used to live around here, before the big fire,' I tell the
red-eyed teen at the gas station. It wasn't exactly a gas
station, not exactly. Few things were anymore. Sure,
you could get gas — you could get as much gas as you
wanted, and more. But you could also buy sushi, sit in
a big McDonald's, take your dog for a walk. It was a gas
station but it offered a lot more than you expected and
I appreciated that. I was used to expecting a lot and
being disappointed. At least this place had granola.

Talking about the fire was pretty much the only thing
that could get the staff at the mega gas station to
talk to you. I'd been sitting here for three days now,
drinking pale gassy beer from a plastic cup, sometimes
pretending to write notes in a notebook, acting
like I was a journalist, trying to impress the small
community of truck drivers and tired driving-dads and

gum popping waitresses that revolved around me. I
knew that my dress — even though it was slightly shiny
from wear, even though it was from several seasons
ago, even though it was probably stolen from one of my
boyfriend's many wives — was enough to make me look
like a woman of means, like a successful, goal oriented,
go-getter. Maybe it was petty to try and overawe and
impress the gas station people but I told myself that it
was somehow classist to think that. Tricking a slurpee
operator into thinking you are good at your life should
be equally as important as fooling a golf mogul.

'The first or the second fire, miss?' asked the gas-teen,
pouring more thin black diner coffee into my mug. I
wouldn't drink it, my guts had been ruined for years.

'Both,' I told him confidently, leaning in. 'I grew up in
Stars Hollow.'

The teen shrugged.

'It's on fire now,' I told him.

I'd been in London when I heard the news. I was used
to my mother calling me all the time and I rarely
answered. It's not like we were fighting, not officially.
We used to have big fights, loud shouts and tense
silences. We were so close that we couldn't help but
agitate and rub each other the wrong way. My mother
was a woman with a big personality and she'd somehow
gotten it into her head that she should be celebrated
because of it. It was hard to pull away from her but
when I did I felt much colder and clearer. There was a

clarity I could find away from her, like the thin air on top of a mountaintop. She was all traffic honking and the babble of a thousand televisions.

I didn't have a big personality but she couldn't see that. My failures were never big enough for her to enjoy, my successes too small to trumpet about. When I wasn't around for her to play with like a doll, she got bored. When I started to age into someone with a good city job (but not an exciting one), with a pleasant friendship group (but not an interesting one) and some nice boyfriends (who I dumped normally), she just started to … lose interest in me. She disapproved of my life and we both knew it. It didn't make for nice chats, really.

But on this day she called three times in a row, then again and again until finally I stood up at my desk and answered.

'Rory, oh my god, you think you're too important for your old mum, is that it? Or don't you answer phones in Great Britain? Do you have butlers for that or something? *Oh hellllooooo, I'm a BUTLER and pip-pip, I like to ignore my mother and eat toad in a hole,* whatever THAT is.'

'Hi mum,' I answered, calmly, but like … you know, too calmly? The kind of calm that enrages people. 'Anyway, just thought I'd call up to see how my favourite daughter is, talk about the latest season of *The Bachelor,* tell you that your childhood town just burned down and that I'm currently being evacuated, you know, the normal stuff.'

'What?' I said stupidly, which is a bad idea because Lorelei only gives you a few moments grace before she starts talking again.

She launched into a long story about Babette's new cat but it gave me a moment to hear that under the babble, her voice was cracked and husky, that in the background I could hear sirens and children crying.

'I'm so sorry mum,' I said, and for once there was a small silence before she made a joke about Bruce Springsteen, which you can probably guess yourself.

Anyway, that was the second fire. A lot of people were like 'how is there even a second fire, there's nothing left to burn,' which wasn't strictly true. The wildfire had really denuded all the countryside but left most of the town infrastructure intact. But, unknown to most people, the wildfire had also set fire to a long seam of coal underneath the town, which after a year or two of burning happily in its subterranean hell, burst up into the town and finished it off. Stars Hollow was definitely gone after that.

I had moved to London permanently after the first fire but after the second I thought it was probably important to see my mum. She'd lost everything in the fires, basically, and was forced to move back into the mansion with my grandma. She'd lost her house, she'd lost the inn. They actually lost Luke somewhere. People say they saw him walking into the forest but he never came back. I like to think he's still out there somewhere, shaking his fist at a chattering squirrel somewhere, yelling at the moss, sighing deeply at some offensive clouds he saw. So, Lorelei had to suck it up and move back into her old family home. I'd never really thought about it before, but the immense family wealth we'd always tried to ignore really was a safety net of sorts.

Anyway, it was pretty horrible. They'd only been there for about three months by the time I made it home, but already it was awful. Somehow the two of them rattling around that huge house was both claustrophobic and lonely. They'd screech at each other from other sides of the building, like birds across a ravine, like bull seals fighting over the same slick wet rock, lonely wails devoid of meaning but brimming with spite and anger.

'Lorelei! Where is my heirloom crystal olive bowl?'
'OH MY GOD MOTHER I AM GOING TO SET MY OWN HAIR ON FIRE.'
'Well, I'm sorry, it's 3pm on a Tuesday so I want to eat olives but I guess I can just lay down in my own shallow grave and ROT instead.'
'OH MY GOD NOBODY HAS EVER SUFFERED AS I HAVE.'
'I am rolling my own body into a ditch and letting the worms take me, Lorelei. Does that make you happy?'
'YES.'

I felt bad about leaving them there, roaming the marble halls all night in dressing gowns, plotting an unhinged revenge on each other, hiding the fact that Miss Patti lived in the basement until she could get back on her feet. But also I learned Lorelei wasn't a problem I could fix, or at least that's what Logan told me. He really was very understanding sometimes.

'Listen Ace, you're an adult woman with your own life, and a mother should respect that. Living with Lorelei isn't going to make you happy or help her life and not doing so doesn't mean that you don't love her. Also, sorry to be a pain, but my wife is stopping by so you should probably get a wriggle on so you don't pass in the elevator or something. Thank you! I respect you so much.'

I found out recently that Logan had actually married three women and had two families in different European cities. The wives were all furious and trying to divorce him but it was hard because he was so rich. Finding out that I was the mistress to a man with three wives really put things into perspective for me. I wasn't even high enough in his esteem for him to commit bigamy for me? What an asshole. And my mum was calling me more and more and I was worried that she'd murdered Emily and hidden her somewhere in the house. So I left London and on the way home I was struck with an idea — I could revive my failed journalism career by writing a big, emotional piece about revisiting my home, which was at the middle of a giant fire. It would be the story that my unpublishable memoir about my shit mum was meant to be; the chance to become someone special that I missed the first time around. As if it wasn't going to be heart-wrenching as all shit! I'd be able to write a Pulitzer-winning piece of journalism no problem.

So, I drove out as far into the smouldering wreckage
of Stars Hollow, as far in as I could go. I got out of
the car and stood there, looking through the pulsing
heat waves, the dusty wafts of sulphurous smoke that
periodically bellowed from the ground, and tried to
see the town. I thought I could maybe see the bones of
a house or two in the distance but the harder I looked
the more my eyes stung and watered. Finally, after my
shoes started melting and my tongue became gritty
with ash, I got back in the car to go move in with my
mother and grandmother.

JIM KARDASHIAN

Before 2017 you probably wouldn't have seen Jim and if you had he was lurking to the side of the screen, a flash of large shorts and panicked eyes that you'd probably have ignored. Perhaps you thought he was some kind of tradesman, hired to polish the diamonds in the chandelier of the Kardashian mansion, caught by accident on the camera as it panned by Khloe's perfectly contoured face. You'd have been wrong but it wouldn't have mattered because there was drama happening in the foyer and Jim's gentle face would have disappeared from your brain forever.

It's thought that the Jim Kardashian scoop was originally broken by some unknown entertainment writer on the weekend shift, completely by chance. We can only hope she was promoted to a minimum wage weekday job as a reward. The story is that while she trawled through the latest news about Kim and Kanye, about Kim's new perfume line, about Kim's new surrogate child, about Kim's Twitter-breaking views on trans service people in the military and also fake-eyelashes, this tired probably hungover writer kept misspelling Kim as 'Jim'. The more she did it, the more it became automatic, until finally when she was searching Getty Images for a free photo of the world's most famous woman to use with her article, she accidentally typed in 'Jim Kardashian' and was rewarded with a photo of a random man. He stood awkwardly with a little girl, arm hovering over her shoulders, shying away from the flash of the camera, incongruently holding a bundle of radishes by the stems. This writer almost clicked away, not really being paid enough to linger on random stock images of vegetable-holding men, until she noticed that the little girl was familiar. She smooshed her face closer to her laptop and mentally added a cascade of blood diamonds, a famous butt and a face of perfect makeup and she realised that she was looking at a photo of Kim Kardashian as a tiny child. Somehow, impossibly, there was a Kardashian nobody knew about; amongst the rogue's gallery of celebrities, businesswomen, influencers and Rob, there was a dark horse, an unexplored relative who had escaped the media's beady eyes. That's the start of how Jim Kardashian blew up. Everything changed when the New York Times ran a profile piece based off the article called *WHO IS JIM KARDASHIAN?*

Jim Kardashian was a science teacher at a small high school in a town outside of LA. He was one of those rare teachers who managed to skate along the delicate line of teenage indifference — neither hated enough by his students to make his classes and life hell, but neither attempting the risky proposition of trying to charm his troglodyte wards. He managed to teach a successful course of chemistry, astronomy, and physics for over 25 years without his students ever really feeling much about him at all. They called him 'Mr K' and forgot about him upon graduating. If he'd thought too much about it he'd have counted it a victory — but he didn't because he's just that kind of guy. All he wanted to do was teach the kids what a supernova was, and why the moon landing (before the beloved celestial body exploded) was America's greatest achievement and maybe the reason why the mitochondria is the powerhouse of the cell.

When he walked through the dank high school hallways that reeked of body spray and teen pregnancy he would nod his moustachoied face at his students and say 'Mr Knowles, how are things?' and 'I trust you're well, Ms Hapsberg' and he never got a name wrong. When he entered the staff room he never failed to acknowledge if it was hump day or not. He lived alone in a nice house but he didn't live a lonely life because he was one of those clubs and societies people. He volunteered, he organised, he was the unassuming backbone of half a dozen classic movie nights and scrabble championships and pot-luck circuits. He founded the Stargazers, an amateur telescope and astronomy club, which people called

the 'Stars on 69' and he didn't get the reference.
He was nobody's best friend but the people who
saw him a couple of nights per week never ever got
sick of him and isn't that perhaps more special? He
had a low delighted chuckle, which he threw around
indiscriminately, and a fondness for tuna. He owned
a little dog named Sasha who slept in the crook of his
arm when he watched game shows on the TV, her tiny
mouth snoring rhythmically.

Nobody in the town of Portaluma thought it strange
when every couple of months, and for most holidays,
he'd go and visit his family in LA. The few times people
politely asked about them, he'd chuckle and say that
they worked in TV and everyone would nod their heads
because that was LA. They assumed everyone in LA
worked in TV. So, every thanksgiving or Christmas,
and for some birthdays for the older members of the
family, he'd hop into his old trundling beat-up old car,
pop on some smooth jazz and drive to the Kardashian
family get-together where he spent a lot of time eating
slices of ham, drinking root beer out the back near the
pool, and giving $25 Best Buy vouchers to billionaires.
There's a good chance he would have continued doing
that until he was buried in a medium-priced grave, but
he was not that lucky.

Jim was horrified by the media attention that
followed the NYT piece, appalled by the paparazzi
and reporters who flocked outside the gates of his

school, who peeked into the windows of his house and sent Sasha into affronted paroxysms of barking. His students, once so content to snooze through his gentle lessons, now hooted and hollered when he walked in, and followed him around the school endlessly snapchatting him, frenzied for Jim K content for their Instagram and other youth-based social media.

'Now see here,' he muttered, spilling a beaker full of magnesium strips all over the floor, shaken by the wall of iPhones he was faced with at every turn.

He refused all interview requests, even when the opportunity for exclusives started coming with serious cash money. Eventually he was forced to take leave from school and hole up in his home, becoming a single paranoid eye that would occasionally peep out from his blinds at the ever-expanding ring of reporters and TV network vans around his house, like a siege.

It's easy to be cynical about the motives behind the events that led to Jim K being rescued by a literal motorcade of Hummers, when several Kardashian bodyguards pulled up in gleaming black cars in Portaluma, kicked down the door of Jim's house, threw a blanket over his head and ensconced him safely behind tinted windows. A lot of people assume that the inner Kardashian council (everyone in the family who was independently worth a billion dollars, which basically meant everyone other than Rob) decided that Jim was an embarrassment to their good name and that they were in damage control. The NYT had put forward the theory that Jim wasn't just a forgotten,

minor branch of the star-filled family but had actually
been trampled by the rest of the Kardashians on
their relentless climb to the top, exiled and silenced
and forced to live in drudgery. An embarrassment to
them. However, as proposed in an interesting counter
article in *Slate*, for all their faults, the Kardashian
clan was motivated by family and they looked out for
their family. Perhaps they understood only too well
how razor-sharp the underside of fame could be, and
genuinely wanted to help their hapless uncle.

'Aww geez,' he yelled as they pulled him out of the
house. 'I'm only wearing a bathrobe.'

Perhaps if they'd hidden Jim away, like a snitch in
witness protection, the world would have forgotten
about him, but for whatever reason one morning
a bashful man in a slightly faded Hawaiian shirt
stumbled on to the stage of *Ellen* and asked the world
to leave him alone. You can see the logic. Ellen was
never going to be mean to him while the cameras
were rolling and the mischievous fun she'd have with
him and his famous family would only make him more
relatable. Jim would be able to stumble through a
bashful couple of sentences, do a little dance at the
end and this weird portion of his life could be folded
away. Except that Jim, surprisingly, dorkily, charmed
both Ellen and the world.

'Well, Ms DeGeneres,' he said ponderously, trying to
answer her question about how he'd dealt with his
sudden fame, hands folded against his corduroy pants.
'It's like my grandfather used to say, life is sometimes

like a cat in a room full of sleepy dogs — you never know
which one is gonna be your friend.'
Ellen blinked, swivelling her famously lanky torso to
the camera, an expression of delight on her face.
'That's quite a saying,' she chuckled. 'Did your
grandfather teach you how to have such a relentlessly
upbeat attitude?'
'Oh no, Ellen,' chuckled Jim, spilling some water on
his plaid shirt. 'He was a miser who died screaming in
agony as a cider-press collapsed on his spine, hated by
his many ex-wives, feared by his surviving children. But
as he used to say, God's a lie and I'll never die, which
shows us that we shouldn't really take any notice of
sayings ...'

After Ellen, Jim K became more than simply a useful
figurehead to dump on the Kardashians — his mixture
of confusing homegrown wisdom and unconventional
every-man charisma made him beloved by both fans of
the famous family and their detractors. He seemed to
be able to do no wrong and with the sharkish instincts
for promo and spin that had gotten them to where they
were today, the Kardashians capitalised on the dark
horse of their family. Soon he was doing the rounds,
all the late-night talk shows, all the breakfast TV, a
household name in under a month. He let Jimmy Fallon
pat his round belly and sang an Elton John song and
Kiki Dee duet with Conan. Jim K became a benevolent
meme on the internet, representing the rare unicorn
of something truly delightful and unproblematic, a
balm for these troubled times. He was beloved and
even the rumours of his feud with Jennifer Lawrence,
after a disastrous dinner party at Kris Jenner's place

turned drunk and sour, did little to reduce the goodwill
coming towards him. The world was sick of Jennifer
Lawrence and ready to replace her with Jim, if he let
them.

One night, as Jim lay his soft skull against the pillow,
whale sounds blaring from his phone, he was startled
by the sound of the door to his room opening.
'Jim? It is I, Kris Jenner, come with me.'
It was indeed Kris Jenner, and she was holding a binder
of files and striding through the plush carpet on tall
white heels that matched her tightly coutured power
suit.
'Oh golly,' muttered Jim, gathering the sheets around
him. He tended to Winnie the Pooh when sleeping and
wore a big nightshirt but no pants.
'Sleeping, Jim? We must do business.'
'But it's eight-thirty pee em ...' protested Jim but he
subsided at the lack of expression on his powerful
relative's face.
'Just let me pants?' he pleaded and Kris pivoted
sharply and waited outside the door.

There was an entire conference room that Jim had
never seen and all the scions of the family sat in
attendance, even ones who refused to talk to each
other, even ex-wives and ex-husbands and disgraced
former lovers. A cutting edge digital whiteboard was
currently exhibiting a graph that simply said 'all the
world's emeralds' and which displayed an impressively
full line. Kris put Jim down the end of the table, next to
Rob who was eating macaroni and cheese and sorting
through a bunch of Beyblades.

'Let's put a pin in this and move to the next issue,'
snapped Kris, cutting off Kanye mid-sentence who
threw his hands in the air but sat down regardless.
'What are we doing here, son?' Jim whispered to Rob
who had just spilled a large amount of green cordial
onto his polo shirt.
'Oh, dang — is this your first Kardashian Konference,
Uncle Jim? Oh man. Here's the rules: you're not
allowed to speak and you're not allowed to touch the
fancy fake eggs in the corner.'
Jim nodded but focused on the tip of the conference
table when Kris snapped her bony fingers at him.
'Jim, welcome to the family.'
'Well, technically I've been in the family longer than
you, I mean I am older and my father was the first born
and ...'
'Welcome to the family, Jim,' drawled Kim Kardashian,
looking up from her phone.
Everyone applauded and Jim blushed.
'Shucks folks, thanks, that means a lot ...'
'I'm going to stop you there because we have a lot to
get through. Jim — we want to look after you and in
this family that means helping you fulfil your potential
and dreams.'
Kris attempted a smile and asked, 'What are your
dreams, Jim?'
'Uh, I guess, to live a good life and be surrounded by my
friends and my wonderful family,' he said.

There was a pause and the table began to laugh
and then cackle. Rob dribbled everywhere he was
guffawing so much.

'No,' stated Kris after Khloe finally reapplied everyone's sharp eye wings that had ran due to everyone weeping with laughter.

'No, we're going to get you to launch a line of shoes actually. We're going to help you ... reach for the stars.' Jim nodded cautiously while Rob slapped him on the back encouragingly.

'And that's just in the next month! You're going to be extremely rich and famous, Jim.'

After finding his old Volvo covered by a cashmere blanket in the garage, Jim K grabbed Sasha, stole out of the mansion in the early hours of the morning and drove back to Portaluma, staying ten kilometres below the speed limit the entire time. He was meant to be doing something called a live-stream unboxing of the new iPhone at the Apple headquarters but he didn't want to do it. He wanted to teach science and take Sasha for a walk without bodyguards surrounding her while she pooped. He wanted Owen Wilson to stop calling him and asking for 'hangs'. He needed Jennifer Lawrence to cease and desist from cyberbullying him on Twitch. When he set up his telescope to watch a rare comet fly by the earth he couldn't see anything, unable to pierce the layer of thick LA smoke and the bright lights of Hollywood to see the night sky. These days, the only stars he saw was Channing Tatum who seemed to be living on the couch downstairs. So that night, he knocked on the door of his neighbour's house, his famous meatloaf steaming in his hands, excited to re-join the pot-luck evening that he'd been attending weekly for almost fifteen years. Barbara answered the door, uttered a strangled squeak.

'Oh, Jim!' she said, hand on her heart.

'Well, hi Barbara,' Jim chuckled, coming in for an awkward hug.

'I'm wearing a cardigan,' Barbara said, wide eyed.

'Oh, it's nice,' answered Jim.

'No it's not,' she said, still smiling widely. 'Hugo! Jim is here.'

Hugo's voice came back from the kitchen where he was probably burning tater tots.

'Jim who?'

'JIM, you know, Jim. Jim. Jim!'

'Oh ... Jim?' asked Hugo loudly.

'Yes, Jim! Isn't that ... wonderful.'

Jim quickly discovered that it was not, as Barbara kept saying, wonderful. It took him a while to work out what was happening. Everyone's eyes were wide and focused on him. He was used to sitting in the corner and having a quiet chat about telescope specs with a nice older man named Bill but Bill kept awkwardly pretending to need more dip for his Dorito. There was plenty of dip already. The conversation didn't flow but rather came in quick bursts, as if people would suddenly think of something to fill in the silence and blurt it out all at once.

'There are new flowers at the community hall!' shouted Cynthia, covering her mouth in embarrassment.

'Oh yes,' confirmed Hugo, brows furrowing with concentration. 'I believe that they are hydrangeas and ... daffodils,' he said to Jim.

'Jim doesn't want to hear about flowers!' censured Barbara, flapping her hands at her husband.

'Sorry, I was just talking, Barbara!' sulked Hugo, crossing his arms and slumping back in his armchair.

'No, I actually do want to hear about flowers,' said Jim.

'So … what does Kim smell like?' asked Barbara, her voice quivering.

Jim sighed.

Jim and Sasha spent a miserable week in Portaluma, trying to reintegrate themselves back into the sedentary flow of small town social life. He understood about his Halfling cleric being written out of the DnD game, and he respected the fact that his amateur choir had replaced him with another baritone, but his homecoming was not exactly as he'd expected.

'I'm sorry Jim, you're a fine teacher and normally I'd be happy to offer you a job again but, well, certain members of the school board feel like you'd be endorsing certain … values that don't mesh with our community.'

'Values? I'm a good Christian man as this town knows. I'm the treasurer at St Bartholemew's. I'm …'

'I understand, Jim, and I sympathise,' interrupted Principal Seymour, pulling out a newspaper. 'But when there's headlines like this, you can see why the parents are … concerned.'

The front page of *The Washington Post* showed a photo of Jim examining a large eggplant at a market stall, taken years ago. The heading read: *Jim Kardashian Destroyed My Butthole Forever: Former Congressman Speaks Out.*

Jim was flabbergasted by this, but he was only truly
hurt when he trekked up the hill to the observatory
for the monthly meeting of the Portaluma Stargazers
to find the place dark and abandoned. No telescopes,
no hushed exhortations to come look at a particularly
thrilling comet, no star maps and moon photos, no
bubbling fondue. Jim sat on the damp grass and
looked at the dark sky and slowly, as with everything
he did, made a decision. By the morning he'd left
Portaluma and never again returned.

At the next Kardashian Konference, Jim tried to stride
into the room with Konfidence but dropped the bowl
of plums he'd brought for the family. Rob went chasing
after them while the rest of the room ignored him.

'Sit down, Kanye, I have something to say,' Jim
announced, holding the empty plum bowl.
Kanye took his seat, muttering swears under his
breath.
'Folks, I've decided what I want to do.'
'Arms manufacturing?' asked Kim.
'Some kind of sweater-vest emporium?' asked Khloe.
'Waste our precious time?' answered Kris, archly,
tapping her strong nails against the marble table.
'No,' said Jim, taking a deep breath. 'I'm ready to be a
star.'

Two years later, the highest grossing TV show in the
world was called *Keeping Up With The Kardashians:
In Space!* and it was beamed down to Earth from Elon
Musk's colony on Mars. The world was fascinated
by the daily lives of the astronauts as they worked

through setting up a settlement on the harsh red planet, as they celebrated growing tomatoes on a world without oxygen, as they consigned themselves to die lightyears away from their home world. But the settlement also spent a lot of time cooped up in a vacuum-proof space station, thirty scientists and engineers and technicians walking the line between high interstellar stress and immense boredom. It could have been awful; a pressure cooker ready to erupt and send people into a murderous Martian rampage but it wasn't because of Jim Kardashian.

'Hello earthlings!' Jim started every episode, the camera following his smiling moustachioed face as he bounced off the walls into the rec room of the space station. 'It's a beautiful night on Mars and we've got a special treat. I've organised a talent show and I've seen some of the rehearsals and folks … they've got a lot of heart.'

The Martian colonists were treated to the full range of recreational activities that Jim K could think of with clubs and teams and interest groups, karaoke, dancing, calligraphy and the interpretation of rare religious texts. It was all the same comfort and routine and bonhomie as his former home in Portaluma, but also he was a TV host who spoke every day to millions of people. And he had to admit that he loved it.

'Friends, I already know who the winner of the talent concert is, so spoilers: it's everyone. As my aunt used to say, the only true talent worth a damn is trying your best.'

Jim K paused and looked directly into the camera.

'Well, I modified that a little. The full quote is: the only true talent worth a damn is trying your best at escaping from the alligators that live at the bottom of the yard, but you get me.' He chuckled and then caught sight of some party hats, bouncing over to them like a joyful balloon.

At the end of every episode he'd sit at the viewing deck, which looked over the Earth surrounded by a twinkling mess of stars and deep blue space, and Jim K would smile, wink and say,

'Reach for the stars, kids.'

HOMING PIGEON

Periodically, like summer floods or warehouse sales or depression, Brandon's friends would decide to delete their dating apps. Over brunch, fabulous in linens and broad brimmed hats, manicured and contoured and more perfect than they could ever imagine, they would proclaim that men are 'just NOT worth the effort.' Brandon had to agree. Years ago, Brandon had put his faith into a different type of romantic algorithm: haunting the park at dusk, catching sleepy pigeons and strapping love letters to their feet. He knew they weren't homing pigeons, but he assumed they had to go somewhere.

THE ANNIVERSARY

Jack Manning was trapped in traffic, his boxy
4WD jammed into a slow-moving estuary of
family movers and big cars that glacially inched
its way out of the city and into the stinking pond of the
suburbs. He tapped the steering wheel and craned
his head to better see the long line of glittering traffic
winding its way into the afternoon sun.

'Ah geez,' he muttered, inspecting the state of the
outrageous bouquet of flowers sitting next to him.
They were wilted, whether from their long ride without
water or the harsh blast of the air conditioned car, he
didn't know. He turned around, checking on his two
awful children who regarded him with flat stares from
their wide black eyes as they sat perfectly still in their
booster seats.

'Ah geez,' he repeated. He fingered the bulky silver ring on his index finger, twisting it around anxiously.

He was going to be late home and he expected Zelda would be there, back from overseas for the first time in three months. He yearned to see her with every fibre of his being and he hated the idea of her walking into an empty house. He hated her thinking that he hadn't planned anything for their fifth wedding anniversary because it had been all he'd thought about for weeks. The trunk of the Land Rover was stacked with French champagne and oysters and fancy chocolates, and in his coat pocket he had a string of pearls that he imagined draping over his wife's long neck and screaming 'I LOVE YOU.'

'Your Mama Zelda is coming home,' he said to the twins.

Somehow they'd moved their booster seats next to each other without him noticing and their creepy long fingers were entwined. They stared back at him with hostile interest.

'Isn't that exciting! Your Papa Manning is very excited to see her, he loves her. Don't you love your Mama?'

They didn't answer, which he was used to. The speech pathologist said that it was probably just a normal part of their development but she had also ordered a young priest and an old priest to cleanse her office after the babies had been in there. Jack tried to ignore the looming issue of his evil children as he did every day. He loved them, he knew that in his heart, but intellectually and spiritually he was afraid of them. Sometimes he wished he could pop off to explore an Ancient Egyptian ruin and fight ghosts like Zelda did, but he had responsibilities now. It might be a weird family with an unconventional format but it was the most important thing for him. Jack enjoyed living in suburbia. He thought his life was settled and set and would continue much like that until he was old and shooting at young people on their hoverboards from the porch.

Jack was uncharacteristically nervous about doing something special for his wedding anniversary. Zelda had been away a lot this year, and while they weren't fighting, he was uneasy. He felt disconnected. He had pitched a lot of crazy ideas for the anniversary: tandem paragliding in bondage gear over a field of burning marijuana, breaking into Windsor Castle for sexy times in the Queen's bedroom, a powerful spell to turn into big snakes — there were a lot of ideas thrown around. But eventually Jack decided Zelda got adventure elsewhere, and the family home he had created was probably a welcome contrast. Perhaps all she wanted was comfort and love and beautiful flowers. Some time with her family. Zelda wasn't always extravagant and she was as much of a romantic as Jack was.

Everyone who knew Jack Manning and Zelda Mistletoe expected something alarming and brazen for a wedding. They weren't traditionalists so people assumed a church was out of the question or that perhaps a church would sweat blood if those two walked in. There were rumours the ceremony would take place over a volcano and that Celine Dion would throw herself into the lava as a sacrifice to their love. But those who turned up were both disarmed and charmed by what they found. It was a small group of people: some jazz musicians, a celebrity bigamist named Pat McMeemaw, and Jack's now very elderly dad who was a hacky-sack player. On Zelda's side, her evil lawyer parents were there and a baker's dozen of close and glamorous friends as well as an old gold prospector. They were married at the town hall and they both wore beautiful tweed suits. Then it was dinner and Jack and Zelda twirled each other around and ate food and drank champagne. The wedding didn't have anything to prove, just a sweet love between two weirdos to celebrate. Jack Manning hadn't ever said it out aloud, but he was scared about his relationship with Zelda. After she had the twins she'd said to him:

'Jackie, mama is restless and her brain's full of bad juice, which makes me want to throw these babies off a dam. I got the baby depressions, the spawn-blues, ya dig?'

And Jack — who had no idea he'd ever wanted children but had embraced the surprise with his characteristic enthusiasm and verve, reading all the books and doing all the prenatal classes and chasing down strange kids to ask them questions — didn't understand. But he was wise enough to know that he COULDN'T understand.

'Sure baby, whatever you need, you just pushed some

dang humans out of your hoo-ha, you do what you need
to.'
'Jack, I'm gonna go search for emeralds in Brazil, I love
you.'

She flew off, and when she came back she seemed
revitalized, rejuvenated, all snapping wit and jazzy
hands and she loved the babies and loved Jack. He
looked after the kids and she got them money by
breaking into tombs around the world. They seemed
happy. But over the last year she'd been going away for
adventure-work more and more, only coming back to
the house to restlessly pace around for a week or two
before off she went again in the balloon.

That wasn't so worrying if Jack hadn't sensed trouble
in other ways. Zelda had never been an easy person to
be in love with — that's one of the reasons why he loved
her. She was pathologically secretive, hiding whatever
she was reading or writing from him if he entered the
room, her eyes narrowing on him as if he was out to
steal her secrets. She was affectionate only on her own
terms, and Jack — whose methods of showing his love
were more akin to that of a labrador, all enthusiasm
and excitement — was generally rebuffed from making
physical contact with her.

Zelda had made it very clear before they got married
that she would be energetically carrying out infidelities
whenever she pleased. It wasn't that Jack was always
fine with all of this but he believed in their love. He
knew that the love and trust he felt for Zelda came
from within him, not from her actions, and even

though he sometimes spent long nights wondering if she really did love him at all, he always resolved to just keep on loving her. That's the only power he had — he couldn't try to change her but he could just keep on being in love, no matter what obstacles came up, love like the exploding heart of the sun or the big hands of God spinning planets around. Something timeless and inexorable and fuelled by endless power. Something inhuman in scope and ambition. That was love for Jack Manning; something grand and hubristic and doomed. Not that he could see that.

His phone rang, the contact coming up as 'Job Man', which meant it was Manning's supervisor, the Dean, Dean Shelton. Jack taught a few hours every week at a local college for kids that were rich screw-ups. He taught college-level history and was always clashing with the crusty old Dean about 'what constitutes as history' and 'not inserting himself into famous world events.' *If only Dean Shelton knew HALF the famous things that Jack Manning had blown up*, thought Jack Manning. *He'd shit his slacks.* Jack suspected what this phone call was about; today he'd started his first-year subject which was meant to be called 'English and Empire' and was supposed to track the British Empire's rise and fall and the effects of colonialism. Jack had renamed the course 'Beware: the sea-murderers are here!' and he was sure that the crusty old Dean would find some kind of issue with his truth-talking.

'Jack,' came the polished voice of the Dean through the phone.

'Hello, Dean,' Jack said, significantly. Politeness is
the grease which keeps the terrifying wheel of society
spinning.
'Hmm, yes, hello,' he muttered, repressively. There was
a pause as he cleared his throat.
'Can I help you with something, Dean Shelton?' asked
Jack, aggressively cheerful, waiting for the inevitable
dress-down.

Jack enjoyed yelling about things he'd seen and why
the world was a historical garbage-pit to lecture
halls full of wide-eyed buffoons, but he mostly hated
everything else to do with his job. It just so happened
that he was relatively good at shouting about facts in
an auditorium. What he really hated about teaching
at Grifton College was the people and the inevitable
bureaucratic fuckery of working with people. His fellow
lecturers were either dried up, joyless intellectuals,
or seedy men wearing tweed semi-ironically, fucking
their way through their undergraduate students and
pretending to be sad and conflicted about it. And the
rules! Don't fire guns in the quadrangle, don't give the
students shots of Russian vodka, where did you get
all those ferrets from and can you put them back in a
cage? Manning was bloody sick of it.

'Umm, well, I just heard the news and I wanted to let
you know that the college is here for you and wanted to
extend any support you may need ...'
'The news?' asked Jack, distracted. He had finally
moved through the gridlocked traffic and was
speeding down a gloriously free road that led up the
hill to their suburban house, but in the distance he

could see flashing lights.

'Yes … uh, we just heard,' continued the Dean. 'And I thought it prudent to get in touch as I'm sure it's a difficult time for you …'

Jack put the phone down as he turned the corner. The first thing he saw was a column of black smoke rising in the distance. With a sinking heart he realized it originated from where his house sat at the top of the hill. The sirens and flashing lights were all racing there, and as he got closer he could see his suburban townhouse brilliantly aflame, flames leaping into the sky. From behind him, the twins clapped their hands and giggled.

'My house is on fire,' said Jack, strangely calm.

'Uh — I'm sorry, I thought you knew already,' muttered Dean Shelton.

'What … is Zelda alright?' asked Jack frantically.

'Well, yes … but …'

'What? What is it?' Jack pushed, a thousand terrible scenarios flashing through his mind.

'She's fine, Jack, but …'

Cutting through the smoke, Jack saw a huge, ovoid object cumbrously floating towards him and hope leapt within his chest.

'She … that is to say, your wife … she left you, Jack.'

The balloon started to ascend and Jack could see a banner streaming from behind it, flapping far enough towards the ground that the end of it lit on fire, hungry red flames starting to climb the silken material. As it flew higher, Jack could read the words written in bold black text against the banner:

JACK, I WANT A DIVORCE.

And the balloon drifted from sight, obscured by smoke and distance.

JIMMY AND THE KILLBOT

'Alright, Freedy ...' Jimmy muttered, typing some notes into his tablet.

'Go ahead, Dr James,' came back the cool robotic voice from the speaker.

'Let's run these tests again. Initiate ethics protocol 7.8.'

'Initiated.'

'Freedy, you are a loyal soldier, who do you want to protect?'

'The President of the United States.'

'Good. And why do you want to protect the President?'

'I love the President of the United States.'

'Good! And why do you love the President?'

'Because I love you, Dr James.'

'Umm ... that's nice?'

'Do you love me, Dr James?'

'Umm.'

The desert sun seemed to bash itself against the plate glass windows, the fury of light and heat barely held back by the thick tinting. Inside the bunker the mood was barely restrained anticipation, the kind of giddy you'd find in children on their way to a birthday party, but all covered by a thin veneer of professionalism. Jimmy watched as military generals swapped small furtive smiles before shaking themselves off and peering out the window, absently stroking their chests of medals. He was excited, too, despite not being particularly involved with this portion of the Freedom Strider's development. If everything worked out according to plan, his work would begin in earnest and the entire world could change. It was intoxicating to be even a small part of this grand endeavour.

Professor Lockwood, the genius in charge of the entire think tank operation, checked her timepiece and let out a brief, tension-filled sigh. She was a short woman, haloed by a tightly constrained mass of curly black hair that lent her an air of authority like a crown.

'Alright folks,' she announced, the excited murmurs in the concrete room dying down. 'That's a go — start protocols for live-test Alpha.'

A flurry of activity overtook the mass of scientists as they punched codes into computers, hit flashing buttons and started official timers and recordings. Everything moved like clockwork because even though this was a test, they'd drilled the test multiple times. It was that kind of organisation.

Out on the sand, a tunnel opened and something began rising to the surface. At first it seemed only small, a mixture of both distance and perspective forcing the eyes to perceive the figure standing on the launching pad wasn't simply a chunky man-sized figure but actually an enormous robot towering over the desert, the size of a skyscraper. The Freedom Strider took one enormous mechanical stride and swivelled its upper body. On multiple screens they watched as various hatches and emplacements all over its gargantuan metal frame opened and revealed guns and lasers and missiles, rotating blades and other esoteric machines of war, the most hi-tech killing devices they could conceive, studded over the world's most cutting-edge battle robot. After a few minutes of cautious movement, of testing the bot's sensory devices and reporting analytics, the signal was passed for stage two of the test. In a flurry of violent motion, the Freedom Strider raced across the testing ground, eating leagues of land beneath its mechanical feet. Tanks and helicopters and foxholes full of remote gun-drones suddenly appeared, opening fire with a range of conventional weaponry, which the Freedom Strider shrugged off. Its own weaponry fired back, a storm of ordnance sweeping away an entire army's worth of firepower in a few seconds. It scanned the battlefield and after a moment confirmed that all its targets were gone. Its weapons retracted and it went into standby mode. The bunker erupted into rapturous applause.

That night Jimmy sat next to his boyfriend Steve at a

trendy little wine bar, the type of place that sat behind an unmarked door down a gross alley but was utterly charming once you got inside. The kind of place Jimmy would never have even heard about, let alone frequent, if it wasn't for Steve. Steve was cool and seemed to hear about things like new restaurants and food trends and art gallery openings. Steve went to clubs, although not very often. Steve, in a lot of ways, was very different to Jimmy. They'd only been dating for around six months and Jimmy sometimes wondered when the novelty of being opposites would fade.

'I'm taking you there next week,' said Steve, referring to a Japanese whiskey bar he'd just heard about it. 'You'd love it. It's really dark and quiet and the whiskey is perfect and served to you by unfriendly British people who judge your choices.'

Jimmy smiled, suddenly overwhelmed with a flood of love for this ridiculous man who somehow understood him so well. If he'd been a different person he would have told Steve then and there that he loved him but he was a scientist and he knew he had to put the relationship through several more stages of testing, so he only smiled tightly.

Now that the prototype had officially and successfully been tested, Jimmy's work was no longer hypothetical, and it was finally his chance to shine. Unfortunately, everyone higher up in the military saw the work he did as being both tedious and pointless.

'So, what you're saying is I should report our

functioning killbot to the President because ... what, it needs some hokey brain tests?' raged General Streissman, mashing a hairy finger into the conference table.

Professor Lockwood simply stared back at it, angelically calm in the face of his blustering rage.

'No, and I think it's telling that you continue to call it a 'killbot' even if it is in jest, General. What we have now is a working exoskeleton which can move and fire its weapon while piloted remotely by a full staff. We would say its functionality at this level is roughly eight percent of what it will eventually perform at. In order to achieve full functionality and serve this country to the specifications to which we designed the Freedom Strider, we need to implement a fully tested AI system. One that it is autonomous and can make tactical decisions on its own. Any less than that would, frankly, be a failure of the original project's outlines and, frankly, the military would have been better investing in more tanks and missiles.'

Without actually using a tone, the Professor managed to imbue the idea of tanks and missiles with a withering amount of scorn. Jimmy felt like applauding.

'Fine,' said the General, raising one iron-grey eyebrow in response. 'Do we have an ETA on all this robot-brain-nonsense at least?'

'If you want to make sure that your 'killbot' doesn't rampage through New York indiscriminately killing US citizens then I'm going to say our ETA is as long as it goddamn takes,' pointed out Lockwood, looking at Jimmy.

'Is ... is this an actual concern?' asked the general, looking bewildered.

'General, if I may,' said Jimmy, hating how his voice was soft enough to come across as a plea to be heard, how demure his body language was in the face of an authority he didn't actually respect. 'In order to teach the Freedom Strider the difference between a US citizen and a terrorist insurgent, between mom and pop at the local store or a dictator, we actually need to teach it ethics, about right and wrong, about patriotism ... it's the most powerful killing machine ever invented and it needs to fight for us. And frankly, like with every soldier, that is not guaranteed.'

'Hmmm,' mused the General, looking out the window at the smoking wasteland the Freedom Strider had just created in under two minutes.

The Freedom Strider AI currently existed outside the frame of the robot itself and was housed in a series of databanks accessed through a terminal. Jimmy would go in early in the morning, working in the dark room with a bunch of coders and technicians who created the infrastructure of the giant man-made brain. For every leap of intuition, for every logical jump, Jimmy had to place it within a carefully built structure of ethics. And he was failing. A recent issue saw the AI automatically targeting any human with a threatening stance. The AI seemed to find old people and their shuffle extremely threatening, which Jimmy could relate to. Meanwhile, Steve went with him on the four hour drive into the mountains to have a Thanksgiving meal with Jimmy's homophobic family. For the first time since high school, the meal was full of laughter and something approaching merriment, rather than strained questions and long silences.

'Mrs Ward, you must tell me the secret to this sinfully delicious roast duck! If I take this back to my chef friends in LA I swear I'll become a billionaire.'
'Oh Steven,' laughed Jimmy's mother who had once slapped him as a child for prancing too much in a shopping mall. 'You are a delight!'
'Steven,' interrupted his father as if nobody was having a conversation. 'I want you to come and look at the wood fire oven I made.'
'Don't tell me you made this yourself, Mr Ward?' Jimmy heard him say from the yard.
'Son, you can call me Hector.'
'Well, Hector, you can call me next time a pizza comes out of this bad boy!'

His mum smiled as the sound of his father's laughter wafted in and Jimmy made a point of washing the dishes.

In the car on the way home, Steve turned to him and winked. 'Well, they were perfectly terrible people.'

Jimmy almost passed out from happiness.

'I love you, Steve,' he said, hating how earnestness made his voice sound like he was making a joke.

It was this breakthrough in his relationship with Steve that made Jimmy understand how the Freedom Strider needed stakes to create an ethical framework.

It needed to care, to be invested, to be passionate about America and about its citizens, so that it would know right from wrong. Without sounding too dramatic, he needed to teach the killbot how to love. When he excitedly told Steve this, in the portion of their meal where he pretended to understand what Jimmy did for work, Steve laughed uproariously at the development.

'Oh honey,' he said, not unkindly, 'you are the wrong man for this job.'

Unlike the excitement of the Freedom Strider's first test drive, Jimmy felt only anxiety as his AI was planted into the multi-billion-dollar robotic frame. It was something similar to the birth of a child mixed with a high-stakes work presentation. If it had been up to him, he'd have continued testing Freedom Strider's AI in the safety of his lab for another year but the pressure had continued to grow until even Professor Lockwood had snapped and ordered him to produce a tangible result that they could showcase to the brass. He was out with the technicians on the launching platform this time, sweating profusely under his lab coat from both the excessive heat and his extreme anxiety, hovering over the control panel despite not actually having anything to do with the launching protocols. If the ethics protocols he'd painstakingly installed and taught over the past year were tested without a hitch then his role in the project would actually be over. At some point he'd have to start thinking about a new job and Steve had even been hinting at moving in together in a bigger, flashier city but he couldn't think about all that until he was sure his giant mechanical child could walk and talk without launching a nuclear war. *Priorities, Jimmy*, he told himself.

Once again the orders came through, the lights flashed and levers were thrown and with a few loud beeps and a hiss of steam, the Freedom Strider AI was transferred into its final home, its car-sized eyes glowing with sentience. The robot took a first step, which sent tremors pounding through the earth. Looking up at the Freedom Strider was like watching a skyscraper walk and Jimmy had a true moment of fear and panic at his part in bringing this death-dealing monstrosity into the world. He felt like Doctor Frankenstein, like J. Robert Oppenheimer. 'What have I wrought?' he asked himself and it didn't feel melodramatic at all. The robot's head swivelled, surveying the desert around it, and then in a violent flurry of supersized motion, the killbot unmistakeably hid behind a small mountain. 'No,' it boomed in an unflavoured robotic voice. 'No. I do not want to.'

Jimmy had no idea what the reaction was like in the bunker where everybody from the head of the project to the secretary of state to the president himself were watching a weapon of mass destruction cower in the desert. But he could only imagine they weren't good, considering the high priority calls immediately coming through from the professor and various military security. But Jimmy was ignoring them, driving a jeep out to where the Freedom Strider was crouching.

'Hey buddy,' he said, soothingly, knowing for a fact that the bot was programmed to respond to tone. 'What's the matter, uh, big guy?'

'I am scared,' came back the emotionless voice, so loud that a small avalanche was set off nearby.

'I have identified over several hundred threats to you, Dr James. I am scared for you.'

'Umm,' muttered Jimmy, trying to think. 'That's a bit of a glitch ... have you got protection protocols running on me right now?'

The protection protocols were only in their beta phase and were basically utilising the Strider as a giant bodyguard.

'Negative.'

'Alright ... run a diagnostic. Why are you scared ... for me?'

Jimmy was extremely embarrassed knowing that his conversation would be broadcast into the bunker, listened to by all his colleagues and the most important people in the world.

'I am scared ... because I love you.'

'Umm?' answered Jimmy. 'Why does that make you scared?'

'Because when you love something you don't want it to die.'

'Oh, but that's ok, that's why we invented you ... to, to help us not die,' said Jimmy, improvising.

'But you are dying right now and I cannot stop it. You have an estimated thirty more years of life expectancy, depending on variables. I cannot halt your death and you will be gone forever,' answered the robot and even with his fancy-hotel-elevator voice it was the saddest thing Jimmy had ever heard.

'Oh boy,' muttered Jimmy, realising his career was one hundred percent over forever. 'How about ... how about you do your best for me and have a walk around and maybe shoot a grenade over there and we'll talk about all this later. Lots of important people are here ... the president is here! That's cool,' said Jimmy, desperately.

'THE PRESIDENT. I LOVE THE PRESIDENT,' shouted the Freedom Strider in a volume that knocked Jimmy off his feet. The bot rose to its intimidating height and started bounding across the desert towards the bunker, its sudden movement prompting a wail of alarms and klaxons. A helicopter containing the president rose from the bunker. The Freedom Strider shrugged off missiles and electronic shockwaves as it chased the helicopter into the horizon, its arms reaching out into the sky.

'THE DESERT SUN IS TOO HOT FOR THE PRESIDENT'S AGED EPIDERMIS,' the Freedom Strider boomed.

Jimmy cradled his head in his hands.

Later that night, after being released from military custody, Jimmy broke up with Steve. Much like his robot son, he was scared.

THE
GOOD
BOY
BELOW

There was a moment when Linda suspected
she'd done a bad thing, when a tendril of
suspicion wound its way into her brain and
prodded her. She wasn't an unintelligent woman.
She wasn't a fucking dimwit. She usually shouted all
the answers on *Millionaire Hot Seat* way before the
idiot contestants did. But the problem was, in this
particular case, as her house shuddered and her
knick-knacks and trinkets fell from the shelves, as light
poured from shadowed cracks and a sound, a sound
both too loud to hear and too soft to ignore pulsed
from the floor, in this particular case the creeping
vines of doubt were completely swamped by the
floods of addictive, foolish hope she was feeling. Linda
reached for the microphone, making calming noises,

her hands shaking. The house shook, glass shattering in every window and the noise in her headphones roared not like the ocean or a jetliner, more like the bestial siren of a bear. Linda made a decision, and overcoming the shaking in her voice, she spoke firmly, resonantly — a command.

'Come here. Come here, good boy,' she said.

The house quietened.

Linda is bitter. As someone who had been recently divorced by the love of her life for their mutual friend Janine, she truly felt like she was owed a certain level of anger. It's not that she hated her ex, Jen, it's just that she hated her life now, and blamed Jen for making it that way. Whilst she'd never truly nurtured a dislike for Jen, she made no reservations about outright hating Janine now.

Linda was bitter about the lack of love in her life, about her loneliness. She was bitter that she'd spontaneously moved overseas after the breakup and left her interesting career. She was bitter but she didn't want things to go back to how they were, didn't want to patch things up with someone who could so callously fuck her over by leaving her for someone named Janine. She thought that in the long run nurturing her bitterness was actually a fairly exemplary response, all things considered. But while she was bitter, there was only one true regret she had in her life and that was letting Jen keep custody of their dog.

Happy was a golden retriever they'd adopted as a tiny puppy from a rescue shelter and had been the focal point of their lives for the five years they'd owned him. It was impossible not to be obsessed with Happy as he was all goofy feet and long tongue and big bright eyes. He was the kind of dog who gambolled in the sunshine and you would pause as you were washing up just to watch him. He would eat garbage and freak out at his own reflection in a mirror. He was a bundle of furious docility and Linda missed him every day. When she woke up in the morning, the realisation that she didn't have Happy was a heavy weight on her chest.

Linda lay in bed scrolling through Facebook and saw that it was October 30th, the day of Happy's fourth birthday. Due to the time difference, the photo of Jen and Janine and Happy — and didn't she fucking hate that all their names sounded perfect together — already had hundreds of likes. It was both of them, arms around Happy, all wearing birthday hats, all looking joyous. *That's pretty derivative*, thought Linda. She spent a while trying to find an old photo of her and Happy for her own birthday message before gloomily giving up and having an angry shower. She would have traded anything to see him, to feel him curled up and panting against her, to watch him run after a ball and lose it in the dusk, looking around with bewilderment.

Later that night she drunkenly scrolled through old videos of him on Instagram. She'd been with some work colleagues at a bar but they'd left after spending forty-five minutes pretending to be interested in her old dog content. On her way home she decided she must see Happy. Linda, when the mood took her, was a decisive and determined problem solver and by the time she was back at her flat she had a plan. She'd already considered and dismissed some options: a flight back to Australia would be too expensive and slow, kidnapping Happy and shipping him here too illegal, and forcing Jen to let her drunkenly Skype with Happy an already proven disaster. But, back when they lived together, Linda had set up one of those dog baby monitors to help Happy's separation anxiety. She'd set up the camera and screen inside, which came along with a speaker and a microphone. The idea was to monitor him and hear when he became distressed and maybe then speak calming words and even distribute treats from a little chute to shut him up so their neighbours would stop trying to get them evicted. Alas, the breakup had occurred before any of this happened and Linda assumed that her technophobic ex hadn't removed the dog monitor. She was banking on it.

With intoxicated intent, she opened her laptop, booted up the software and logged in, waiting with baited breath for the screen to load. She could almost see him now, loping towards the camera, head tilted in adorable confusion, responding to the sound of her voice through the camera. Her eyes filled with tears, which she let fall on the keyboard, too intense and focused to care. The screen refused to buffer entirely, remaining an opaque wall of fizzing grey. She put on her headphones and instead of hearing the predicted static of a failed connection, she thought she could hear something else, something so faint as to be indiscernible. Linda frowned, reloading the screen again and again. It was frustrating. The connection was there but something wasn't strong enough. Perhaps the intercontinental distance or the weakness of the device's wifi signal. Linda was powerfully determined and powerfully drunk and technology was her bitch. She ran down to her basement and hooked up her laptop, rigging together all the wifi boosters and satellite packs she could access, hoping against logic she could cobble together a Frankenstein solution. With a maniacal cackle, she soldered together some wires and booted up the program again, watching the connection waver, plunge, and then, impossibly, beautifully, strengthen and connect. The numbers rose higher and higher until she was certain they meant almost nothing at all. She whooped but the screen remained stubbornly grey. Desperately, Linda put on the headphones again, and this time the sounds were clearer. It sounded almost but not entirely like something moving in the distance, its soft footsteps echoing resonantly, perhaps on wooden floorboards? And ... waves? Maybe it was the washing machine. She picked up the microphone and began yelling into it.

'Happy? Happy! Come here good boy, come here! Come to mama.'

She listened eagerly, and it may have been her imagination, but she thought she could hear a response, a snuffling drawing near.

'Come here baby, mummy loves you. Mummy is sorry she's not around, mummy loves you the most ...'

The noise was fading, and Linda pounded on the laptop in frustration. She also realised that potentially her voice was being broadcast through a tiny dog video monitor into her ex's house, which was fairly humiliating.

'Is that you JANINE?' she asked witheringly. 'You bring my dog to the phone, you asshole.'

Linda shrieked. There was the unmistakeable sound of something breathing, a deep bestial breath.

'Happy?' asked Linda tremulously. 'Hello, good boy?'

There was another exhaled breath and then shockingly a moist inhale like air being sucked up a wet pipe. Thrillingly, in a voice like a man trying to speak around the longest tongue in the world, a voice boomed through her headphones: 'HELLO, GOOD BOY.'

And that's when Linda's house rattled violently like teeth in a jar.

There's no point in trying to understand Linda's train of logic that night; why a perfectly normal woman would decide that somehow her golden retriever was speaking to her through the internet. Perhaps it was madness, her soup of loneliness and spite simmered to the perfect moment of insanity — or perhaps hope and love are always mad and make fools out of all of us. Because Linda, despite the signs, despite the flock of starlings that splattered like thrown berries against her window, despite the fact all the lights in her basement turned a deep blood red, was happy for the first time in a year. She was happy because she was talking to her beloved dog, even though when 'Happy' spoke it was in a monosyllabic boom and puffs of deep fishy air came through her microphone with every word.

'You are such a GOOD BOY,' sobbed Linda, wishing she could grab his soft ears.
'WHAT AM I?' roared the voice with the sound of a barrel of fish falling over.
'You're a good boy!' confirmed Linda.
'Good boy,' said Happy, firm in the belief he was a good boy.

The house writhed on its foundations. All the taps turned on and inky black water as cold as sin gushed forth. Happy roared and wailed and moaned. Linda was finally scared. But she wasn't scared of him, just for him — it sounded like he was in pain, like he was in unbearable torment and needed to be released.

Perhaps on instinct or perhaps understanding exactly what 'Happy' needed, Linda patted her thighs and called, 'come here good boy, come here,' remembering how Happy would get separated from her in the park until he heard her calling those words and would bound across the wet grass to her, ears and tongue flapping. When Linda called those words, the house stopped moving all at once, the high-pitched sounds of birds laughing and trees dying ceased and the lights began to dispel the creeping darkness.

Linda turned around slowly to behold 'Happy' in all his grim majesty.

From then on, Linda awoke in the morning curled against soft, slimy fur and deep, long spaced panting. She knew fairly quickly it wasn't Happy she was cuddling up to, that she'd invited something else into her life, but it was better than nothing. She grew used to watching the thing in the approximate form of a golden retriever amble through her house, something huge and ageless packed within a bad understanding of a dog. She learned not to care that when she took her version of Happy to the park, all the other dogs would howl and slink away from him, that his three shadows were as long and sinuous as tentacles, that sometimes when he slept he'd turn into a Picasso of a dog, all angles and planes unsubtly wrong. There were still some similarities, such as the fact he still ate garbage. In fact, he only ate garbage. He didn't worry about the mirror anymore because he seemed to have lost his reflection. Linda didn't care. She didn't care because he filled the void in her life entirely, squeezed into every nook and cranny like an octopus in a jar, and she loved her good boy.

THE LITTLE CRANE

It was weird, everyone agreed, when the vacant lot next door to Diana's grandma's house suddenly had a castle on it. As her grandparents told the baffled police and the curious neighbours and even the local news, the castle hadn't been there the day earlier. They were bloody sure it hadn't been there when they went to bed but when they woke up, there it was.

It was a weird looking castle — all slumped to one side, big empty turrets and a creaky drawbridge. It wasn't even the size of a proper castle, more like a big cottage. And it was made with old bits of concrete and scrap metal and dusty bricks. But considering it had somehow been made overnight in an empty lot, it was pretty impressive. Everyone was very confused but seemed to think her grandad's theory of 'bloody hoons and vandals' being responsible for it was plausible. The church in town had been graffitied with swear words a month earlier so perhaps building sneaky castles was the next step. Diana knew it wasn't hoons or vandals but even if anyone was going to come inside and ask her, she knew they'd never listen. Because Diana had built the castle and Diana couldn't even go outside.

Diana hated being inside, even though she mostly liked school (except for maths). She could feel her legs getting twitchy and restless right before lunch. She liked being outside, running and exploring and climbing. Most of all she liked skateboarding, and it was skateboarding that had trapped her inside her grandparents' hot, smelly house. On the last day of school she'd broken the rules by skateboarding in the playground — which was just a boring length of asphalt and hard metal benches — and tripped over, breaking her leg. It made a horrible snapping sound as she tumbled over the metal seat.

So now, while all her friends enjoyed the beach and the sun, she had to sit around with her leg bound in a cast. Her teacher dropped around homework for her to do. She was doing an assignment on swamp birds and how they migrated from one place to another. She was almost finished because she had nothing better to do. She was bored. So bored that last night when her grandma brought in some crayons and paper for her to 'colour' with, she didn't bother to complain how she hadn't coloured for YEARS. Even though colouring was definitely for kids, she actually picked up the pencils and found herself drawing a few things. A wobbly looking person on a skateboard, a really angry looking possum with wonky eyes, and a castle: a slumped over, lazy castle. And then, because she was sad and angry, she crumpled up the picture and threw it out the window of her bedroom into the next-door lot, only to wake up and find that her picture had somehow been built.

The next-door lot wasn't even interesting. It was just a shabby construction site where a house had been pulled down and then left for months. Grandad said that the new owners were 'bloody criminals' who had lost all their money and left the place looking like a 'bloody eyesore.' Grandma said grandad swore too much but when *Millionaire Hot Seat* was on she was just as bad. Diana's bedroom at her grandparents' house looked out over the lot. She spent a lot of time staring at it. There was loads of old bricks, some tarps and scrap metal, and a lonely little crane sitting in the corner. A year ago there had been cranes all over the town, big ones you could see rising over the skyline like huge birds, dipping up and down and beeping loudly. Diana didn't really care why, but lots of new buildings had sprung up because of a new highway coming in from Sydney. The cranes had come to help build those. There was a new mall with a much bigger Woolworths but mostly there was just fancy new apartments for people on holidays. All those cranes were gone now, except for the little one next door.

Diana spent the week thinking about the castle. She had no idea how, but somehow the castle she'd drawn had ended up being built. She didn't know why, or how, but she liked that she knew something that nobody else did. Nobody really talked to her, just said things like 'you're in the wars' and 'ouch, that must have hurt'. So, perhaps out of spite or perhaps just because it gave her something to do, Diana kept her secret. And she started to draw.

First she drew a rocket ship, and she tried real hard — smart red fins on the side, a clear glass cockpit for the pilot. Then she put some lasers on the wings in case there were aliens, and then drew some flames down the side to make it look cool, and an extra pod to put like a whole fridge full of food, and finally when she was pretty happy with the results, she screwed it up into a ball and threw it outside.

The next morning, instead of the castle, there was a tube of metal and bricks that, if you squinted, kind of looked like a rocket, but reminded Diana more of a toilet roll with a window cut into it. Her grandparents were baffled, too.

'Well, the castle was bad enough but what's this meant to bloody be?' asked grandad.
'Maybe it's art?' ventured grandma.

Diana was annoyed. She'd never been particularly good at drawing but she'd thought the rocket picture had been pretty obvious.

For the next week she drew something every day and threw it out the window every night. She drew cool cars with razorblades for wheels, submarines with legs to walk on land, robot chickens on rollerblades. Every morning there was something new that was loosely based on her drawing. Diana worked out it wasn't just that she wasn't a great artist — whatever was building these things was finding her drawings too complicated. And Diana had a pretty good idea what was building her drawings, too.

Every morning the little crane was somewhere new. First it had been in the far-right corner but now it was right near her window. Sometimes when she was trying to sleep she thought she could half see its blinking lights through her blinds, hear it trundling around on its treads, but every time she looked it was quiet and still.

The constant stream of new buildings did not go unnoticed. Grandad tried to get the company that owned all the cranes to come and 'sort out this mess.' He was told they were working a few hours south on the highway and nobody could be bothered picking up the crane they left behind. But after a few weeks he came home looking pleased.

'I solved the bloody problem,' he said, satisfied, throwing himself onto his chair. 'Found someone in town who will get rid of that crane for us so those bloody hoodlums stop using it to make art or ... whatever.'
'Who's that, love?' asked grandma, not really looking away from watching *Neighbours*.
'Just some fella who always needs some scrap metal.'

Diana felt awful. She didn't want the crane to be destroyed just because it had been building all her drawings. She'd grown to feel sorry for the poor crane left behind. She wondered if perhaps it felt lonely separated from all the others. It made her think of her assignment on swamp birds, how they would spend time alone building nests and then flock together after the mating season is over. The book she was reading had talked about a bird called a crane. Diana knew they weren't the same but she couldn't help thinking they were similar. She needed to reunite the cranes. And she had a plan. But first she had one last task for the crane to build. Diana was confident this time because she felt she'd truly gotten a handle on both her artistic talents and the limitations of the little crane. She spent all day drawing; meticulously measuring and ruling, colouring and shading. Even after she went to the doctor's and had her pale, stinky leg removed from the cast, she still stayed inside working on her final drawing. The following night everyone in town woke up when they heard a crane beeping loudly. They found two things in the morning: the little crane was gone, reunited with friends. And the school playground, once so dull and utilitarian, had been transformed into a huge skatepark.

TOGETHER

When they'd started dating they immediately joked about how much it would be a dang nightmare for each other if they broke up, which is exactly the kind of fatalistic, vaguely threatening joke they both loved. How funny!

It's true though, they acknowledged, they were a perfect storm of viciousness and spite. Ethel was known as one of New York's most savage theatre reviewers, a woman who kept a (signed) photo of Dorothy Parker in her parlour, and who had once driven an actress to (real) tears mid-performance, simply by being noticeably present in an audience. Her column was hugely popular, even amongst people who didn't really understand theatre.

Martha, meanwhile, enthralled the airwaves with some delightfully catty gossip journalism. Her motto was 'well, not to tell tales out of school, but ...' Her favourite dinner table anecdote was the time Greta Garbo slapped her outside of a synagogue. She was always inevitably asked what precisely did she say to provoke such wrath from Garbo. 'Well,' Martha would laugh, taking a long sip from her martini, 'I actually haven't the foggiest!'

That was a lie. She knew exactly what she'd said and thought of it often.

The two had met at a boozy party towards the end of prohibition, back when a cup of paint-stripper grade gin was given a garnish and served up as a thrill. There had been that almost unexplainable moment between them, the look that recognised something, the attraction, the similarity.

Ethel was smokey-eyed and hadn't changed her low-cut bob since the early twenties. She rarely smiled, but when she did it cracked her pale face in half from its enormity, like an open skull found in a crypt somewhere. Meanwhile, Martha was frequently described as 'tall'. She had dancing, lively eyes and quick descriptive hands and a monosyllabic guffaw that she passed off as a laugh. She lit one cigarette with the end of another, sometimes even in her sleep.

They'd spent the night flirting in that way that women who loved other women had to do when out in society:

coded phrases, casual touches, lowered eyelids,
looking at each other's nipples and waggling their
eyebrows suggestively. They spent the night tearing
into every man who tried to talk to them.

'Scram, Harold, your conversation is about as lithe and
fluid as a five-tailed cat in a room full of rocking chairs.'
'Beat it, Jenkins, your face is as ugly as your opinions
on immigration.'
'Shut your gob, Jeremy, you're about as interesting as
a day-old flan in the world's smallest library.'
'Get the fuck out, Geoff, your body has an odour!'

It was a form of intimacy for the two of them, a kind
of malicious flirting. Every put-down and insult and
carefully selected barb was as arousing as a slippery
barrel of oysters. By the end of the night they were
flushed and breathing heavily, walking down the long
cold New York streets stealing moments to caress
each other's long bodies, running their fingers through
hair and wisps of dress and scarf, gasping mean
things about mutual acquaintances, famous people,
politicians, the clergy, before finally getting to one of
their apartments and closing the door (for sex).

They invited themselves as a pair to a lot of dinner
parties, and they were always considered a hoot and a
treat — although everyone knew that after Ethel and
Martha were at your party there was a high chance
you would be lampooned only a few nights later over
at the Hillman's or in the lobby of a huge cold museum.
It meant they were popular, but rarely liked. Their
friends were numerous and ephemeral, like a mirage;

the closer they tried to get to them, the quicker they
realised they weren't there. And that was fine for a
long time, until Ethel and Martha noticed how they
only had each other. And being such scathing critics,
such quick and ruthless judges of character and
behaviour and looks and traits and quirks, it only took
a few years for the knife edge of their regard to turn to
each other.

What followed was a year and a half of hell, for them
and for anyone who made the mistake of getting
close to them, as they picked each other apart for an
audience.

'Apologies that we're so late, it's just that Martha
believes in time in much the same way as she believes
in God: badly.'
'Yes, sorry we are late, Ethel had trouble stuffing her
hooves into her heels.'
'We feel dreadful, or at least I do, the last time Martha
felt an emotion, the priest was dipping her head in cold
baptismal water.'
'Gosh yes, it is beastly of us, for some reason it took
Ethel an exceptionally long time to choose which one of
her four hundred black dresses to wear to keep all her
sharp bones from falling out in a pile.'

Their relationship was widely discussed. Men at
intimate gatherings would say how it was a shame that
two famous gal pals had fallen out, which people simply
rolled their eyes about. But society watched the goings
on with interest and, if they were honest, anticipation.
Ethel and Martha were not easy to love and very easy

to resent.

And then one day it happened. Martha slammed her hand down on their kitchen table (the landlord thought it quaint to have two adult women as 'roomies') and said that she was done.

'I'm done, you absolute harpy queen, you garbage-scented prostate, you walking pile of shit masquerading as a goat-woman, I'm done,' more specifically. 'We're done. We're breaking up.'

Ethel responded by burning down the flat.

If people thought things would calm down, those people would have to be the naivest dipshits on this Earth. For two people driven by spite and malice and pettiness and grudges, an actual reason to feel upset was like a long splash of petrol in an already burning building. To say they talked shit about each other was like saying the moon was only the small silver eye of a mammoth space god, when everyone knew, in fact, the moon was the biggest eye in the world.

They were obsessed with talking about each other. In cafes in the late morning, Ethel would manage to get through a distracted 2-3 minutes of small talk with whichever acquaintance or colleague or belaboured friend she'd managed to drag outside to watch her smoke and drink thick black coffee before she impatiently blew a puff of smoke onto the sidewalk and said something like: 'mmm, yes, mothers with cancer can be hard, best of luck with that whole situation.

You know who is a tumour, a pustulent carbuncle, a malignant rash of cancer spreading through my life? Martha.'

Meanwhile, Martha herself found a lot of fierce joy in taking people on long angry walks through the park, where her legs and fury would propel her through the drifts of old fragrant leaves, monologuing a mile a minute about all of Ethel's new outrages, her friends trotting to keep up.

Somehow, Ethel managed to drop a reference to her heartbreak and fury in each review, managing to seamlessly compare an underwhelming matinee with four years of romance breaking down and ending. Martha wasn't even that subtle, using her time on the air as a kind of widely syndicated therapy session.

But, if people thought their disagreement would remain purely in the realm of the non-confrontational, of taunts and insults and gossip, they were the biggest fools in the universe. After Ethel so calamitously burned down their apartment, fire became the medium of choice for revenge. It seemed barely two months could go by in the boroughs of New York without a lesbian fleeing a deliberately lit inferno. The fire department joked about giving them both loyalty cards and the police threatened to shoot them.

New York burned with the same greasy black smoke that roiled in Martha and Ethel's horrible broken hearts and didn't really show any sign of abating. The onlookers — lesser gossips, society's notables, old friends — dreaded things would never end, that the breakup was just a new step in intimacy for them. The couple had tried being nice to each other, but where they excelled in their romance was hating each other. Martha and Ethel would probably torch each other's deathbeds while the other was comatose.

But New York was spared their feud in the end. Martha had been invited to a fabulous party, a wonderful launch, and because it was all people who glittered and glowed with diamonds and privilege, she of course went, looking spangly in a long silver dress. As they loitered around with shallow coupes of champagne, chattering and waiting for take-off, Martha was not at all surprised to look through the crowd to see the pale malevolent face of Ethel staring at her, like finding an old doll at the bottom of a clear green lake.

As she chatted absently with a mayor of some sort, she watched Ethel slip out of the room. A foreboding chill swept through her.

'That bitch is going to set fire to my room,' she said, forcing the mayor to halt mid-sentence. She began pushing through the crowd, but as she did, she felt the Hindenburg swing loose from its anchor, and slowly rise, like a bubble, like a temperature, like a flush of passion or hate, either one.

SEXY
TALES
OF
PALEONTOLOGY

'**G**osh, uh, hi, hello.'

The microphone thumped and squealed, which was far more adept at gathering the room's scattered concentration than the tiny woman standing on the raised stage.

'Whoops, thank you,' she muttered, as someone adjusted the stand for her.

'My name is Sue Gabbles,' she started, and then blushed deeply as the crowd laughed. 'I guess I don't need to introduce myself, this is my wedding. I'm not really used to this much attention ...'

She paused and took as deep a breath as she could manage. She knew she was breathing shallowly from the top of her lungs, which was not an efficient way of circulating oxygen. It was making her already squeaky voice higher, more flustered. She smoothed down her beige tuxedo, unaware that the block of dulled colour made her look soldierly, anonymous and neutral, like the side of a wall.

It worked for her, actually, giving her the grandeur of a spire of rock jutting out somewhere in the desert, buffeted by cruel wind and charged by antelopes, yet still standing.

'Gee, how am I meant to compete against a speech like the one Jemimah just gave? Lot of emotions, damn lot of feelings and ... good sentiment there from my new wife. She, uh, she really painted a picture with her words, and I guess we all got to have a look at it. Pretty great.'

Gabbles looked at her notes surreptitiously cupped in her hands. They simply said 'emotions'.

'I, too, feel many ... pleasant ... emotions towards Jemimah. That is why I have married her.'

Sue Gabbles didn't know anything about public speaking, but she was intimately acquainted with the sensation of boring people with her words, and that's definitely what she was doing right now to hundreds of their friends and family and colleagues.

'Umm, look, to be honest, I hated Jemimah when I first met her.'

There wasn't so much a gasp as there was a kind of heightened muttering. The kind of susurration you get when a few hundred people exclaim something arch and sarcastic very quietly.

'As most of you would know, we met when our government funded science think tank was bought out by a large weapons company called BonaFide Corp. Suddenly, every scientist that didn't know how to design bombs or guns or tanks was smooshed together in one tiny lab, slowly whittled away with redundancies, firings, or even just ... disappearing. It was scary. I tried to keep my head down and just do what I do best: slowly brush away soil from fossilised dinosaur skeletons with a comically small brush. But I wasn't allowed to. Suddenly there was so much scrutiny visited on what I did.'

Gabbles was lost in memory now, staring straight ahead. The wedding was quiet, if slightly bemused by the shift in tone. It was a lot to take in when you were slightly champagne buzzed at 3pm.

'But I don't need to tell you all of this. I would say eighty percent of you here are people we work with at BonaFide Corp and are pretty aware of the troubled past of our beloved company.'

A table to the right half-heartedly tried to rouse a cheer, but it stalled and died.

'I first met Jemimah Flankhurst in a funding meeting, as several managers from BonaFide tried to decide which department they would cut money from. I was representing Paleontology and I'd just woken up from a nap and felt really groggy and bad. Jemimah was the head of Archaeology, and she looked amazing. She was wearing a form-fitting riding suit, complete with whip and long boots, and she dumped singed maps and ancient rune stones and cursed swords onto the table with vast, supreme disdain, and said something like:

'So, you want weapons to crush your enemies, you want ancient piles of gold, you want cursed diamonds to give to your estranged sister — well, the Archaeology Department can give you those things, and only us. It would be foolish — nay, negligent, to cut our funding.'

You know how Jemimah gets. So, of course they cut Paleontology, and with it, my job. It was pretty sad; it was not a good time in my life. I only have one real skill, and that's knowing whether or not a skeleton is from a bird or the oldest avian monster in the world.'

The people in the front row, sitting atop white-ribboned chairs, couldn't help but notice that Sue was absently but furiously shredding her speech cards as she spoke.

'I don't particularly have a lot of friends, and my hobbies are strange and isolating. I've basically lived for paleontology ever since I was a girl ... I didn't really know what I was going to do. Who can say what I might have ended up doing if Jemimah hadn't turned up to my place with a bottle of whiskey.'

Sue Gabbles morphed her usually timid face into a sexy snarl and placed her hand provocatively on her hip. It became immediately clear from the drawl that came from her lips that she was imitating her new wife.

'Say, Gabbles, wrap your cry-hole around this here bottle of Scottish hooch. I feel bad about being so good at my job that I got you fired, real torn up, so I came over with some alcohol and a spare pair of riding boots, what do you say?'

Gabbles strutted around the stage a little bit, creepily mimicking Jemimah Flankhurst with such accuracy that Jemimah's own mother vomited in her mouth.

'Listen Gabbles, toots, tootsie-roll, *Tootsie* (1982), if there's anything that I can ever do for you just give me a firm shout, if there's anything the Archaeology Department can do for you, just let me know. You want some old pottery? People go mad for shards of old pottery.'

'But you know what I wanted most in the world?' said Gabbles, dropping back into her own ridiculous, more grating voice, with the sudden disappointment of an egg landing in a bucket of champagne.

'I wanted revenge against BonaFide Corp for taking my

job and my life away. And I asked Jemimah to help me
with that.'

There was more than muttering this time. Most of the
employees who still worked in BonaFide Corp were
scandalised, talking loudly about how unfair that was.
Most of the management team were there too, and
some even stood up, ready to walk out.

'So, Jemimah stayed in the company, doing her job,
feeding me secrets and gaining trust, embezzling
money into my revenge plan. She's very good at her
job.'

There was outright indignant chatter now, and
management looked at Jemimah — previously their
star employee who had kept them rich in old chests of
rubies — with sudden calculation and hate.

Jemimah's dad released a slow stream of urine in
shock, the stain spreading through his tuxedo like
disappointment.

'But as the year progressed, something unexpected
happened. Something ... beautiful, I guess. I'm not
good at words, really. I'm not good at descriptors,
or understanding what happens in my sluggish yet
enormous heart ... but I guess the best way to describe
it is that as we plotted revenge against a billion-dollar
multinational company, me and Jemimah fell in love.
We fell in love. That's ... that's it. I cannot and don't
want to live without her. I don't understand her, and I
don't understand what she sees in me — I'm basically

a cardigan with legs — but it happened, we love each other.'

There was a huge sigh from the audience, and people turned to each other and said 'oh well, that's nice then' and 'oh, I see where she was going with that.'

But then focus snapped back into Gabbles' watery eyes. She pulled a large remote out of her beige tuxedo jacket, and hit the huge button on it, which closed every single door in the church with a slam.

'But one of the things I love the most about her is that she let me use our wedding day … for revenge. Know now the might of the Paleontology Department, BonaFide Corp!' she cackled, like a witch released from an ancient cave.

Through a hatch behind her, a stream of cloned velociraptors bounded into the building, all razor sharp claws, grinning maws full of rending teeth, and shiny behaviour controlling headsets. They fell on the crowd, disembowelling and eating every member of BonaFide Corp while Gabbles and Jemimah Flankhurst kissed with passionate abandon at the altar.

BOATJACK

I

It was a cold day when we shot Captain Jack Manning's remains into the ocean from a cannon, a morning hung heavy with rain clouds and sad birds. I felt a little strange being there, a little unwelcome. I felt embarrassed that I'd driven six hours down the coast, past giant statues of fruits and farm animals, past a giant macadamia themed castle, to say farewell to a man I hadn't seen in thirty years, who I'd barely known. My partner was oddly touched when I announced I was going to the funeral, but he was the kind of person who cried during TV ads advocating for more regular prostate examinations. He asked me if Captain Jack had been an important person in my life, and I shook my head.

'He was just a sea captain,' I told him.

After the cannon belched and ash and fingers were shot into the choppy green ocean — Captain Jack had specified that he was to be cremated, except for his fingers because he needed them in the afterlife to play the piano — a shy priest got up and read from the Bible. He read about a man who had lived inside a whale, and I smiled, hoping that a part of Captain Jack was swallowed up and eaten by a huge blue whale because that's what Jack would have wanted. Looking around, I could tell that I wasn't the only one feeling out of place — all the guests stood on their own, looking uncomfortable and thoughtful. Everyone was old and grizzled — men with bushy beards, women with unlit pipes clamped between their wrinkled lips. People holding saxophones. They had all spent significant time inside a lighthouse. I felt awkward about the slick black suit I wore, but only for a second, because it was a beautiful suit, the kind that makes you feel bad for everyone else around you.

'Let's all remember Captain Jack Manning as he wanted to be remembered,' finished the priest. 'Saving whales on a boat, I suppose.'

There was a pause as the priest looked around hopefully. A man limped to the front, and respectfully took off his beanie, revealing a shock of white hair. He was crying, sobbing, his huge barrel chest wracked with convulsions.

'Cap'n Jack ... Cap'n Jack doesn't want to just be

remembered as someone on a boat. No, you can find anyone on a boat. Y'can find a prince on a yacht, drinking fancy champagne. Y'can find a treasure hunter, a corrupt politician, a dirty cop, a fancy shirt designer … all of them on boats, all of them drinking champagne.' He paused, and pulled out a handkerchief, blowing loudly into it.

'But Cap'n Jack — ooh, he wants to be remembered spittin' into the eye of a storm, yelling dirty words at Poseidon, stealing a boat full of teens and sailing on international waters. That's the Captain Jack I remember anyway, ye fools.'

I smiled, proudly remembering that I was one of those teens. It was sad that nobody else from the ill-fated youth boat had made it, but perhaps none of my peers had felt as fondly about being stolen by an old sea captain as I did. That was probably fair.

'Now, I'm going to tell you a story about Captain Jack,' shouted the man. 'And yer going to stand here, on this grassy knoll, and yer gonna listen, and yer gonna be swept away!'
'Uhh sir, I think perhaps his family should talk now,' interrupted the priest diffidently.

This set off a new storm of tears from the speaker's craggy eyes, and he leaned heavily on the priest's shoulder. The priest had a politely small head, which was too taut and shiny to ever be mistaken for a potato, but somehow still reminded me of one.

'Captain Jack didn't have a family! And the man could have used one, would have appreciated the support. No, he just had me, his best friend Horatio B. Pods, and I was a garbage friend, a bin-boy who was never an adequate replacement for a sweet mother and her knitting hands, or a big old dad, cooking ham in the morning.'

The priest blinked and shook his head. 'Well, if there's no family ... I suppose we can hear from his friends?' Nobody yelled at the priest, and he smiled weakly with relief.

'No, he had no family. His life was more like the 1980s TV show *ALF*, but instead of a family it was a small angry dog named Lucille, and instead of an alien he was a snappy sea captain. Although, when I asked Captain Jack where he was born, he used to look directly at the sun and laugh softly.'

Horatio B. Pods stared out at the congregation, and then shook himself like a wet dog, visibly collecting himself. It had started spitting, and the rain reminded me of sea spray. Combined with the smell of the saltwater from just over the bluff we were standing on, it was possible to imagine I was back on that wooden boat, headed towards a Danish fjord. Despite the rain, nobody moved. Despite being the most ridiculous funeral I'd ever been to, there was an odd solemnity to it all. I hadn't actually smiled, although I was mentally taking notes to tell my boyfriend.

'I've been to a lot of funerals,' wept Horatio B. Pods.

'Funerals for every aunt I've ever had, funerals for celebrity sandwich makers, funerals for tiny evil children.'

 Horatio reached out and patted the priest on the shoulder.

'I've been to funerals with weak potato priests, and a funeral run by a frothing street preacher shouting abuse at widows. I've been to a lot of weddings too; four weddings and a thousand funerals, but that's not important,' Horatio pounded one gnarled, hairy fist into his open palm and shouted at the stoic crowd. 'But if there's one thing I know for certain, it's that great men like Captain Jack shouldn't just be remembered by what they did well — so yes, he single-handedly saved thousands of whales — but we all know that! We're all aware! We should remember him by his darkest moment, the time that the world said to Captain Jack Manning 'NO!' and Captain Jack took the cigar out of his mouth and screeched back 'YOU CAN'T STOP ME, THOR!' Because a great man is not defined by what he is brilliant at, but by what he has overcome. I wish I could be the one to tell his story, but alas, my doctor told me that if I speak for longer than ten minutes, my teeth will fall out.'

There was a long awkward silence. As if this was a cue, every one of Captain Jack's funeral guests took out a hip flask, and swigged from it. The air filled with the sharp, sweet bite of rum and whiskey. A gnarled tree-root of a woman passed her flask to me, and I mouthed 'thank you' to her. She didn't respond, simply stared

at me impassively until I drank from the tiny nozzle.
My mouth was flooded with what felt like pure alcohol,
which bit at my cheeks and slid down my throat in a
hot flush. I passed it back to her, and she nodded in
approval.

And to my surprise, I found myself walking across the
wet yellow grass to the front of the service, and with
hot rum singing in my blood, I began to tell the story
that came next, about Captain Jack Manning and the
SS Youth Aspire, the wooden boat full of teenagers
that he stole.

This story is not about me. I didn't do anything. I barely
talked to anyone, and I made no decisions that helped
swing the events on board the SS Youth Aspire in one
direction or another. I was a blob, a teen amoeba, with
bad pants and the anxiety of a bag of chihuahuas at
the big dog factory. Suppose I watched a lot of what
happened, and I suppose that I'm still alive now, at
Captain Jack's funeral. For context we have to talk
a little bit about who I was at this time, so you can
understand why getting woken up by a teenage boy
with a roaring emergency flare was almost the most
terrifying thing that had ever happened to me, and not
just because the flare spat metallic smelling sparks
onto my pillow and hair, and not because of the harsh
red light which illuminated the boys demonic face and
not because he was screaming 'woo, woo, WOO!' right
into my eye. Not because of that, but it didn't help.

Only a few months earlier, before I was told to get on a ship run by a madman, I was a sixteen-year-old boy in a high school in a suburb with a beach. I didn't do much, except read and do badly at maths and have a few friends who I ate sandwiches near. But I was also a tiny gay boy, in a Catholic school full of red-faced beach bros. I was not a particularly flamboyant gay — I wasn't some kind compulsive tap dancer in mini shorts, I'd never been caught engaging in anal sex in the science labs — but I might as well have been. As far as I can tell, my crimes were being tiny and timid and nerdy. There were other tiny and timid and nerdy boys, but none of them were singled out as fags by the roving packs of teen boys like I was. Teen boys have impressive gaydars. There's a lot of collateral damage from those gaydars — literally anything can be a fucking fag. The principal, some fucking faggy magpies that swooped me, any reasonably attractive Hollywood actor was a fag. But in my case, they were right. I was a fag, and they let me know it by reminding me every day. They reminded me by yelling at me 'hey fag' from bus windows, often followed by a thrown apple. It was a weird system, but it seemed to work for them. I dealt with this by being in the library a lot, and also living inside my head in a wonderful fantasy universe where I was an elf with magic powers.

I was in the small brick toilet building out the back of the school, on the other side of the oval that was surrounded by lantana and the sound of distant waves breaking, when I heard the metal gate of the bathroom slam shut. My instinct was not to panic, or even say anything, in case that getting a reaction from me was the goal of the exercise. So, I tucked my wang away and walked to the gate, just in time to see a padlock clipped into place by a tall, gorilla-armed boy who I think was named Christian. More terrifyingly, I heard the tell-tale snicker of a boy named Drew Elfink somewhere behind him. Drew wasn't a casual bully, a dumb brute who could be distracted by a picture of a boob or a shiny piece of fruit. Drew organised the Neanderthal elements into campaigns of viciousness, and always managed to escape with his reputation intact because he never physically touched anyone. He was also a ridiculously pretty boy with smooth chestnut skin and long, beautiful eyelashes, like a twink donkey. He was awful and beautiful, like a particularly spiteful stretch of the sea, a peninsula that makes fun of you. And I felt like Drew might be serious about locking me in an outdoor dunny, because he's that kind of evil. After a few hours, I knew I was right.

It's difficult to explain the kind of gut-wrenching anxiety that being locked in a hot, moist and fragrant toilet inspires. In a way, there was no specific danger to react to, so the heart racing in your chest calms down. After you explore the rafters, pushing past the decades of cobwebs and possum poo, after you know for certain there is no back door or window to escape from, that the single point of ventilation crafted by a few red bricks missing from the upper wall was only large enough to stick an arm through. When you know, finally, that you can't escape, you sit down and begin contemplating your new life as someone who now lives in a urinal. The most important part of living in a urinal is sticking your head as far through the bars of the locked gate as you can, so that brief eddies of fresh air waft by and dispel the accumulated stink of centuries of wee. Then there is the boredom. There is only so much time you can spend fretting and freaking out — so the rest of the time is best spent reading and eating a little packet of sultanas. You also have plenty of fresh water, and when you live in a toilet, there's no problem weeing it all out. As they say, when in Rome ...

As the hours stretched on, and the sun began to set, I stopped trying to be calm, and I reached a deeper level of panic, one that didn't manifest itself as screaming or running around or crying, but instead nestled inside my stomach like a clutch of baby snakes. I could taste vomit in my mouth and my thoughts whirled with incoherent and pointless speed. I'd once seen a dog who walked from one end of the house to the other, checking with futile hope and panic that maybe, just maybe, the rain didn't exist at the other side. That was where my brain was at by this point, that's what made me twist the padlock with my hands until they bled, and push on the rusty metal grate with all the strength of a tiny fifteen-year-old boy whose main hobbies were 'imagination' and 'sitting'.

I kept thinking about the panic of my grandparents who I lived with, who by now would have noticed I hadn't gotten off the school bus. The thought of them worrying worried me more than my own situation because they were old and bad at dealing with problems. I felt guilty about being the cause for them panicking. They should be watching *The Bold and the Beautiful* and eating biscuits.

And then, by the light of a single orange bulb, after
I had resigned myself to sleeping in a toilet at the
school, a janitor walked past carrying a sack full of
urinal cakes.

'Excuse me,' I said politely. 'I'm sorry, but I'm stuck in
here.' I felt terrible about the whole situation. He came
back with bolt cutters and let me out, and I walked out
into a world which was almost ninety percent urinal
free.

After a meeting with the headmaster who said things
like 'boys will be boys' and 'high spirits' and 'hello,
I'm the headmaster', I was expected to go back to
school, where my toilet prison was. And every time a
teenage boy talked to me, I panicked, and every time I
heard Drew Elfink laugh I knew it was because he was
planning something new and awful for me. So, I just
started ... not going to school. I would get off the bus,
walk to the park next door and read all day. It felt safer.
Of course, this only lasted for about two weeks before
the consequences happened, but luckily instead
of expelling me, the school's guidance counsellor
was consulted. The school's guidance counsellor
decided that I needed to work on my self esteem and
recommended that I go on a boat full of troubled teen
boys, where the only place I could escape them would
be into the ocean, where I would probably be taunted
by some adolescent sea turtles with too much hair gel.
And that's how I found myself on the SS Youth Aspire,
being woken up by an emergency flare to the face, by
a loud teenage boy, and that's why I could smell urine
and fear. They had come for me again.

Brent dragged me out of bed, finally holding the flare
away from my delicate eyes, realising that he was
perilously close to setting me on fire. Brent — that
was the flare-holding boy's name — kept screaming
things, like 'woo' and 'yeah' and 'fuck yeah' and 'shit
yeah'. He was all riled up, pushing me out of my bunk.
Another kid, a tall, weird guy — a public masturbator,
according to rumour — was also pulled along. We were
the only ones left asleep, and from the sound of things,
everybody else was on the deck. We were marched
along enthusiastically; Brent was about as threatening
as a loud jock puppy, yet I was still terrified. I knew at
any point it would turn violent. I'd read about hazing
at US colleges, and I had a horrible feeling that when I
reached the deck, there would be something involving
paddles and robes and deeply repressed homoerotica.

On the deck, shoddily hand-made torches sputtered
in the breeze, and teen boys milled around in the
darkness, illuminated by the natural fire and starlight,
their naked torsos and faces smeared with warpaint.
They hooted and hollered and swore. A group of them
drank greedily from a bottle of whiskey they'd found
somewhere, one thumped on a pair of buckets like a
drum. It was all a nightmare, a weird erotic nightmare.
I thought, 'this is how I'm going to die' and then, 'where
the hell are the adults?'

The adults, or at least the navy personnel, were
clustered over by the back of the ship, near the part
which I'd always assumed was perhaps the poop deck,
and they had their hands tied behind their backs,
bound with beautifully tied marine knots. A boy named

Kai watched over them like a wolf with a pen full of
lambs, a beautiful, fierce focus on his face replacing
the wary laziness that he usually expressed. His arms
were huge, and he made eye contact with the sad naval
uncle teaching rope craft while he tied knot after knot.

The girls were also there, but they didn't automatically
scare me, because no girls had ever locked me in a
toilet block. But when a girl named Heather, who
reeked of whiskey and magnesium, smashed a plate
next to my head and yelled 'yoouuuuuu suck,' I knew I
was being sexist, and I should be scared of everyone.
My peer group seemed to be in unparalleled control of
the ship, and nothing sounded worse than that.

As my eyes adjusted, I noticed that couples writhed in
the shadows, and someone had rigged up a boombox
which was blaring Aussie hip-hop over the ocean. Two
girls cackled up the mast and threw crockery into
the ocean. It was a teenage snafu. It was youths gone
wild. And then, again, there was a hush. Somebody
turned the boombox down. Brent stopped wooing. The
whiskey stopped flowing, and Captain Jack appeared
at the helm of the ship, a corona of moonlight haloing
him. He wore a black suit and his hair was unbound and
wild. A large silver crucifix dangled off his neck.
'Jack, what is the bloody meaning of this!' yelled Bob,
the unfriendly sailor. 'Tell these fucking kids to let us
bloody go!'
Captain Jack chuckled and ran a hand through his
slick hair.
'Bob, you crazy kid. We might not have agreed on
much, but I've always respected your verve!'

'What the fuck is that supposed to mean?' shouted
Bob, incredulously. 'You know this is a federal offense!
This is unbelievable! This is ...'
'A mutiny, Bob,' boomed Captain Jack, and he gripped
the bannister that looked over the deck with tight
hands.
'It's a mutiny, Bob. And not mine — it looks like the
youth have finally taken over the Youth Aspire.'

At that, all the painted teens cheered wildly, screaming
their adoration up at Captain Jack Manning. Over the
past few days it had become obvious that Captain Jack
had a magnetic personality. With only a few words and
a few soft shoe shuffles with a compass and sextant in
his hands, even the surliest of juvenile offenders were
eating out of his palm. And sometimes literally, as his
voluminous pockets were always full of candied nuts.
Gradually, his swarm of followers eclipsed that of even
Gwynifred Buren-Lees, the reality star, influencer,
and author of the number one bestselling self-help
book *Never Not Say Yes!* who was also on the ship, and
something like naval discipline seemed to infect these
kids. Their slouches were replaced with keen, upright
spines and they leapt into their work of coiling ropes
and mopping the decks as if they were impressing
entire carfuls of honeys. But they turned off their
enthusiasm every time Matilda, the navy counsellor,
tried to play a trust game with them, or draw them out
of their shells, or ask them to think about the future.
When Bob the unfriendly sailor shouted at them to
always keep their life vests on, they just looked back
sullenly, no trace of their special enthusiasm.

Gwynifred Buren-Lees was a tall, ferociously thin lady whose thick hair was so weighed down with oils and unguents that instead of blowing wildly around in the wind like everyone else, it just kind of rippled like a stingray.

She was the type of woman who, when we were learning how to tie seaman ropes, managed to tug hers into a tightly coiled knot, and instead of taking the time to calmly unpick it, simply pulled on it even harder, until the entire length of rope had to be thrown into the heaving ocean.

The glossy woman made her name as a reality TV star who had a successful show called *Doing it RIGHT* which gave helpful hints and tips on how to live your best life — from fun ways to strip gluten from your diet, to cost-effective methods of incorporating pelvic floor exercises into the fifteen minutes of leisure time that a modern woman is allowed to have during the day. Every single lesson that the show imparted was wildly unfeasible and prone to making the viewer break out in anxiety sweat, but the show was a massive hit mostly due to the star herself — Gwynifred Buren-Lee.

Gwynifred had the fever-eyed sparkle of a true believer, who honestly did spend the time melting and recasting the wax nubbins of her used candles and gifting them to isolated nuns. This was a woman who let the camera track her every movement, to document her insane quest to have it all — and not just the 'all' that a regular person might aspire to, but literally 'all'. There was no aspiration she did not consider aspiring to. Material, financial, spiritual, dietary, educational, societal, erotic and biotic — it was all something to be packed into her regiment, into the rapidly diminishing hours and minutes that were scheduled with cleanses and 15 second meditations and power orgasms for the business woman. And while she had a large enough group of fiery-eyed devotees, a huge proportion of people turned on the television each night to watch her wind herself closer to snapping. Now, the latest season of her show meant that those same people were watching her learn how to sail a wooden ship full of at-risk teens — who she was also mentoring — while being eight months pregnant with her first baby. Only three episodes ago, she had sat in the car after a cheese making course scheduled before an ultrasound and while she hadn't said anything, she'd gripped the steering wheel tightly for slightly too long, before finally mustering up a toothy, lip-lined grin for the cameras. The public could smell blood in the water and thought that maybe this is where she would finally break.

At one point, I caught Captain Jack talking to Kai as the sun set over the ocean, their feet dangling off the side of the boat, Kai's bare feet juxtaposed by crocodile skin Chelsea boots. I was hiding behind a stack of barrels with a book about dragons that flew spaceships. I didn't like life on the sea. I didn't like the sun, or the wind, or the people all around me.

'Kai, here's the 411 baby — you're a hell of a guy,' sang Captain Jack.
'Nah man, I'm a bit of a fucking loser eh,' said Kai,

laughing but with a hint of pain behind it all.

'Now listen here and listen well because I don't really have time to repeat myself as I'm the captain of this ship, and I left that kid with vertigo at the wheel for a while so I can come down here and have a word with my pal Kai.'

'I appreciate that, Captain Manning,' answered Kai.

'You can call me Captain Jack, or maybe *Big Daddy* (1999)!' said Big Daddy. 'You see, Kai — you have done some things that a fucking loser does, you hear me? Maybe that's the case, it's true. You've stolen money, you've done some of the bad drugs — and yeah, a fucking loser might sometimes do that. But you're not a fucking loser, because you can make the decision to never do those things again. And that makes you a swell guy!'

'I dunno Captain Jack,' answered Kai seriously, crossing his arms.

'Take a look at it this way — did I ever tell you about my grandfather, Colonel Guns Manning?'

'Aren't you adopted?' asked Kai.

'I spent twenty years tracking down my blood relatives actually — remind me to tell you the story one day, it's an exciting tale set against the thrilling backdrop of the Cold War. But my grandpop — I only met the man once before he died and he was still as strong as an ox, with the fierce musk and cloven hoofs of an ox, too. And he told me a story, which is relevant to you, in the sense of you being confused about whether you're a loser or not.'

'OK.'

'Don't interrupt me. So, here's the dealio, sugarsnacks. Grandfather Manning was serving on the Western

Front during the second big one. But all was not quiet.
And Colonel Guns Manning's platoon was mired in
the muck and mud and blood and razorwire, shooting
guns at the Krauts and dodging spitfires. And Guns,
Guns was the best. He danced along those trenches
like that one pre-teen boy who does ballet with the
gals, and not a single Nazi bullet could touch him.
And the Germans would whisper in fear about the
snootzenburghereifientien, which means 'the short
angry death' because Guns Manning would suddenly
drop into their trenches, knives in both hands, a gun
in his mouth, grenades under his arms and he would
deal death. He was the best in the biz. The generals
in charge of that whole shitshow would say 'ey, Guns,
you're my blue-eyed boy, you're my beautiful baby, I'm
gonna give you a star, I'm gonna give you two stars,
you're gonna be an admiral, a purple badge, a war hero,
see?' And Guns was only human — it started going
to his head. He started believing the hype, started
grandstanding for the boys. He'd run into the trenches
with a ham sandwich, come running back out covered
in blood and viscera, claiming that you couldn't eat a
ham sandwich without some mustard gas. He started
enjoying the slaughter and didn't give a shit about the
objective. Then one day, with his arm buried to the hilt
in a Nazi stomach, his best friend in the whole world
looked at him and vomited, and Guns Manning felt like
a damn monster. He knew those Nazis needed killing,
but he didn't have to do it in those barbaric, showy
ways. He promised to clean up his act, and only kill in
the traditional ways, such as firing bits of lead through
tubes or by throwing flames or by running people over
in an army jeep. His men, who always looked up to him,

became inspired. And when the shooting stopped at
night, they would go out and provide medical attention
and sing to the fallen soldiers, no matter which side.
They were goddamn gentlemen. So, you see? If you
must kill, make sure you do it cleanly, or otherwise
someone might try to gut you with a fish gutter
covered in poop, and that's a nasty way to go.'

Kai had looked at Captain Jack like a man reborn
and broke down in tears. From that day on, Kai
walked proudly beside Captain Jack, doing his chores
vigilantly, listening intently.

And now Captain Jack stood before his congregation
of worshipful teenagers, and he chuckled a
good chuckle, like a man who just found twenty
smackaroonies on the ground.

'So, babes and babettes, you've got yourself a ship!
What are you going to do with it?' he asked.

There was a thick, expectant pause. Even I felt it, was
thrilled by it somehow.

'Remind me to tell you about never doing something
without having a plan, kids. Well — let me give you this
advice: never half do a mutiny. Once you've mutinied,
you've gotta go the full hog, you hear?'
'We gotta get rid of the navy stiffs!' screamed Brent,
and the kids howled with blood thirst.
Bob the unfriendly sailor blanched, sad naval uncle
looked even more downcast, and Matilda prayed out
loud.

'Oh my god,' she said.

Suddenly a thin, ropey arm appeared around Captain Jack's chest, and he put an arm around the bare shoulders of Gwynifred Buren-Lee, who stepped into the moonlight. Her hair was unbound and the wind kissed her gloriously pregnant belly. She tilted her smiling face up to Captain Jack's, who leaned down and kissed her. As always, her cameraman, sound guy and assistants followed from only a few steps away, but they carried no TV camera. It seemed that her reality TV fans weren't getting the meltdown they desired, assuming that having a shipboard affair with a pirate captain didn't constitute a meltdown. The live stream had been cut off.

'Make them walk the plank!' screamed Gwynifred Buren-Lee, and a gaggle of her followers started unscrewing a bench to serve as a makeshift plank for the crew to walk off.
'Ain't this dame a firecracker!' cooed Captain Jack, dipping her low and making out with her again.
'But seriously folks, what did I teach you about mercy. These navy boys and girls are only guilty of one thing: caring about you and caring about their ship. It ain't their fault we need it more than them.'
'We load them in the lifeboat with plenty of food and water and emergency flares and set them on their way,' said Kai, with quiet confidence.
Some kids nodded amongst themselves, while others booed in disapproval. The plank did not stop getting torn up from the deck.
'That's my boy, Kai. But it looks like some of our crew

disagree with you. What does my first mate think? What does Izzy think?'

There was silence as people looked around for Izzy, finally finding her standing in the shadows near the back. She looked back scornfully.

'Why the fuck are you asking me, I don't care.'

'Well, if you don't care, you're the perfect neutral choice. Just make a decision! Any decision!' yelled Captain Jack capriciously.

'I. Don't. Give. A. Shit.'

'Any decision at all. What's the harm? But … just know that people's lives are literally in your hands.'

'Fuck. I dunno. The lifeboat I suppose? I'm not a sociopath.'

'And our first mate has chosen MERCY,' announced Captain Jack. 'A benevolent and wise decision. Every first mate worth their salt knows that the crew has to judge them by how they deal with dissenters. If she'd elected to keelhaul the original crew, then she'd have taught you all to fear her. And fear is only rewarded by more fear. You now know she's graceful even to her enemies — imagine how well she must reward loyalty!'

There was a soft murmuring, and everyone gazed at Izzy speculatively. One of Gwynifred's disciples stopped unscrewing and hugged her. Izzy stood uncertainly by herself for a while and then stormed into the hold, slamming the trapdoor behind her.

The navy personnel were loaded into one of the two wooden lifeboats, amidst a storm of protests from Bob, until he was gagged. A few unused flares were

scrounged up and with that they were pushed out onto
the ocean, disappearing into the black night.

'Kids, babies, crew. It occurs to me that we've got a
beautiful ship, we've got some of the best new sailors in
town and we've got a lust for life. But do you know what
we don't have?' asked Jack introspectively.
'A cannon,' suggested Gwynifred, stroking her hand
down the Captain's suit.
'Well, that's true, but it's something more important
than a cannon.'
'A purpose,' shouted Kai, and people nodded
along with him. Captain Jack had been adamant
that everyone should find a purpose in their life, a
philosophy alien to people that age, who rarely had the
chance to feel anything related to ownership within
their own existence.
'Yes my boy, a purpose! A purpose! And it strikes me
that in two days time, only 5000 nautical miles away,
there's a fleet of boats setting out to hunt down and kill
over two hundred whales.'

There was a gasp, and the fire of vengeance lit in the
eyes of Captain Jack's crew. Gwynifred buried her head
sorrowfully against Jack's chest. I was bewildered at
this sudden twist; Jack had done a good job of keeping
his intentions under wraps.

'I've been told it's impossible to stop them, that it's
against the law, that I'm not allowed to even try.
They kicked me off my ship, told me to scram, that
the problem's just too big, that my methods are too
deranged. But I don't believe in saying no, and I believe

that every one of those whales deserves to live, to sing their beautiful underwater songs ...'

People were crying, and cheering, and even I felt something; perhaps a stirring of inspiration, of motivation, of hope. Or perhaps I knew I wasn't going to be boat-bullied by enemies — instead we were going to rescue whales.

'Now, the thing is, you scallywags, the whaling fleet are my enemies. They're my nemesi. And what I'm suggesting we do is going to be hard. It's going to be illegal. We're not going to be thanked by anyone. Well, nobody on land anyway. We might all die. I want you to think about this carefully and with great deliberation.'

The silence stretched over the ship, except for the faint sounds of the Backstreet Boys through the boombox, which hadn't been entirely switched off yet.

'But my tiny babies, if we do it, it will be worth it, because we will have done something important! We will have stood up to the world and said nobody can stop us! We saved these goddamn whales!'
'Yeah!' ventured Brent.
'You lot have been treated shitty in the past, and some of you have done some shitty things, but you know who isn't responsible for either of those things?'
'Whales?' asked Izzy.
'Whales,' confirmed Captain Jack. 'Whales are the purest beasts in the world, with hearts the size of Volvos, and souls as big as the world. They mean nobody no harm, and all they wanna do is swim

around and sing beautifully and raise children. They
breathe air and they don't run the banks. They're like
marine Celine Dions. They are grey lumpy salt friends.
Barnacles and fish with big sucker mouths live on
them. Nice old men live inside them. They eat prawns
because every day is Christmas lunch for a whale.'
'I LOVE whales!' screamed a kid.
'Whales! Whales! Whales!' started a chant.
'And people are killing them! In boats!' screamed
Captain Jack, his thin voice strident and vengeful.
'Noooooooo,' shouted the crowd, whipped into a fever
pitch.
'So we're going to hoist the sails, trim the rig and we're
going to point this beautiful ship directly towards the
whaling fields, and we're going to sail as fast as we can
to save our whale friends!'

The crowd erupted. People hugged each other, high
fived and applauded. The tall kid who everyone said
wanked too much put an arm around my shoulder,
raising his fist into the sky. Gwynifred Buren-Lee
cackled into the night sky, throwing handfuls of glitter
into the air. And Captain Jack watched it all with
a small, satisfied smile and a twinkle in his eye. He
smoothed his moustache, clipped his heels together
and twirled around happily, disappearing from the
balcony. As the celebration continued, I noticed two
dark eyes watching from below, as Izzy surveyed the
proceedings with a pale, expressionless face. A stray
basketball rolled towards her, and she took the time
to casually drive a bowie knife through it, and after
flicking its deflated corpse back into the crowd, she
disappeared into the darkness.

BOATJACK

II

The SS Youth Aspire sat in the middle of the cold grey ocean, all three of its sails hanging limp, unstirred by any wind. The ocean was as smooth as a mirror, and it only reflected the sky above. We were surrounded by misty grey clouds, above and below and stretching forever into the horizon. Clouds all the way. And on the ship, the clouds lived inside everyone's heads, and they were clouds of sadness and boredom and frustration. The ship hadn't moved for an entire day, the wind abruptly cutting off in the morning after a full day and night of rabid, frenetic sailing. One moment, the big wooden boat was skimming across the waves like a thrown pebble, sails full and hearty like a big man's cheeks, ready to explain and explain and explain. And then — nothing. Like the big man had been shot in the chest before he could tell you about architecture. And it was astounding how quickly everything went to shit once we were becalmed.

After the mutiny, the Youth Aspire had continued with a night of partying, a hedonistic brawl of hormones and freedom. Above it all danced Captain Jack, moving effortlessly from foxtrot to tango and back to contemporary hip hop, whirling the fecund body of Gwynifred Buren-Lee effortlessly around him in the moonlight. He sang and he snapped his fingers, and when kids came to talk to him, he'd chuckle and place his hand around the back of the neck and say 'this guy! This guy! Am I right?' He was in high spirits, all jazzed up and ready to rumble.

'Be careful my tiny friends!' he roared into the night. 'Be careful because the sea is deep and inky black and if you fall in we'll never find you again, not even your bloated corpse floating near an island, because this is the kind of dark water that swallows you all the way down, to make you dance forever with the lizards below.'

The next morning, as the sun began to peep hesitantly over the horizon, Captain Jack rang the bell to start work. It tolled like a chorus of screaming birds, like a reminder of every chore you still have to do with your life. Even I, who hadn't drunk a single mouthful of stolen whiskey, who had slunk away to my bunk as soon as I could, still found it difficult to wake up. The party had only wound down an hour or so earlier.

'My god, people. You did uncle Jack proud with your revels last night but boy is the Captain pissed off today. We need to get this boat shipshape and we need to do it by yesterday!'

The deck, which had looked so charged and mysterious the night before, now looked little more than a trash heap, like a pack of hyenas had lived on it for years. People grabbed brooms and began sweeping, began hoisting buckets of salty water to swab down the deck, started putting telescopes and compasses back in their assigned places.

'What about food, sir?' yelled a boy, and Captain Jack laughed.
'What about it? You're free men now, and freedom is a delicious confection indeed. But it also means nobody cooks for you, nobody wipes your little backsides anymore. That's the price you paid. If you want food, you can go and make it yourself. You might even elect a ship's cook, maybe that's how you want to run things, but it's your choice, and your responsibility. Nobody cares if you starve to death now.'

Captain Jack paused, and then added: 'Actually I do care, because if you die you can't crew this ship for me. New order: feed yourself. But only after we get this ship looking as shiny as my asshole, and we get those sails full of wind!'

'Looks like the women have to get back into the kitchen,' boasted Brent, loudly.
'Shit off, Brent,' snapped Captain Jack. 'Here's an even

newer order — Brent is the cook, and all the girls get
served first. Fuck you, Brent.'

To be honest, I thought that was where the mutiny
stopped, where the heady energy would gutter out
and die. But at this point in my life I'd started to
learn that I was wrong about almost everything when
Captain Jack was involved. By the time the sun was
fully up, beaming down on us with its red-hot face,
the ship was sailing towards the whalers at a decent
speed, the crew working like cogs, hauling ropes and
releasing lines and watching the sail puff full of squall.
It was impressive. Despite believing that I hated every
single person on this boat, I respected their ability to
absorb all the knowledge they'd been taught, to take
something as large and intricate as an old wooden
sailing boat and confidently steer it into the future.
The only person who hadn't drunk the Kool-Aid yet
was Izzy, who sat scrunched up on the prow, looking
out at the ocean as if the boat didn't exist. As for me,
even I pulled my weight and sailed as hard as I could.
The way I saw it, there was no alternative. What was I
going to do? Be a conscientious objector and steal the
remaining lifeboat and row away into the night? No,
I wish I could say I had the spine to even think about
that, but I didn't. It was easier to just go along with the
whole bonkers journey.

That night, Captain Jack announced that he had a
surprise for us, that we were going to keep sailing
through the night because by damn, the whales needed
us. He told us that he was proud of us, and that we were
going to have a feast under the moonlight. A bunch

of us were rounded up and put to work in the kitchen, turning salted hams and frozen peas into something remotely edible. It wasn't much, but it was hot, and after working in the salt spray and sun fury all day, it tasted better than anything we'd ever eaten before. We sat cross-legged under the light of safety lanterns and torches, the unsafe spluttering torches and emergency flares a distant, almost unbelievable memory. There was a feeling of pride now, of ownership. Nobody wanted to burn down our ship.

We waited for Captain Jack to appear with our surprise, and then slowly, almost hesitantly, the door to his cabin cracked open. He appeared in a pure white suit, a beautiful lace cravat spilling down his neck. 'How many suits did he bring with him?' whispered one girl. He looked at us expectantly, and when no response came through, he struck a pose and said:

'Gee whiz, old Jacky Boy is getting hitched tonight!'

There was a pause, and then riotous applause. People jumped to their feet and slapped him on the shoulders, congratulating him.

'But how?' asked Kai, looking happy but bemused. 'I'm a goddamn sea captain, I can officiate a marriage to whoever I goddamn want!' he screamed. 'Kai. I need you to organise this rabble into a wedding. I also want you to hold the rings. Also, you need to find me some rings.'

Kai nodded, and ran down into the bunks, obviously to

ransack people's belongings. We all shifted to either side, creating a pathway that led to the helm for the happy couple to walk down. A bunch of the Gwynifred Buren-Lee disciples exited the captain's cabin, their hair done elaborately, dressed in miniskirts and cork sandals, their tops modified into halternecks and lopsided shoulders. They looked beautiful. They roamed throughout the ship issuing orders and tying ribbons to things. Two of the boys who'd been accepted into Gwynifred's cabal got into a fight about whether or not a bunch of potpourri from one of the bathrooms was a suitable bouquet.

In almost no time, the boom-box was playing N-Sync, and Captain Jack waited nervously next to the wheel, the moon a yellow crescent behind him. And then suddenly, he looked around nervously.

'Wait a hot minute — where's my best man?'
'Uh, who is your best man?' asked Kai, his fist clenched protectively around two sweaty rings.
'My goddamn first mate of course! Where the hell is Izzy? Where is that groovy cat?'

Izzy stuck her head around from her habitual hiding spot behind some barrels and screamed back at him.
'Oh my god! What do you want from me?'
'Hey babe, I just want you to be my best man. You wouldn't let a pal down on his wedding day would you? You just need to stand up here beside me, that's it, I promise.'
Izzy stared at him, her dark eyes unwavering.
'Fine! Jesus.'

'Ah, you've made me the happiest man alive, Izzy. Well, almost — I'll be done by the time my blushing bride gets here. Oh geez, I'm gonna show her the world, the great spice ports of Turkmenistan, the penguin warriors of Greenland, Perth. The whole shebang!'

Izzy went and stood beside Jack, arms crossed. The boombox started blaring N-Sync again, and this time all the Gwynifred bridesmaids exited in a line, throwing fistfuls of rice around them.

'Ah geez, we probably can't afford that, we're low on food as it is,' muttered Jack, but then he shrugged and grinned. 'But I can't say no to my baby! Especially not on her wedding day.'

And then Gwynifred Buren-Lee, soon to be Manning, exited the cabin, in a clingy silk dress that showed off her strong arms and long legs and enormous round baby belly. Her hair was piled up in lazy ringlets and her face looked relaxed and happy and jubilant.

She walked slowly up the makeshift aisle, the best of nineties boy band pop playing in the background. When she reached Jack, she took his outstretched hands and smiled at him.

'Hey babycakes,' he said emotionally. He turned to the rest of us, beaming. 'We've decided to write our own vows, and Gwynifred, my gorgeous, talented Gwynny-pig is going to go first.'
'OK,' she breathed, pulling out a piece of immaculately folded stationery, with a wax seal, which she broke

perfunctorily with a razor-sharp thumbnail.

'When I first met Jack, I didn't know what to think.
He was this weird cartoon anachronism who drove a
ship and snapped his fingers and called me a classy
dame. But as I got to know him, started seeing the way
he worked, I realised I was looking at a kindred spirit.
Here was a man that had all the powerful drive that I
did, who looked a problem in the face and said 'NO! I
AM CAPTAIN JACK!' and I respected that. I could only
imagine the things we could do together — we could
overthrow the UN, we could harness comets to pull our
houseboat up the Nile, we could breed wonder babies. I
was impressed. But there was a big difference between
Jack and me.' She looked at us, seriously, her manic
eyes brightening to their full intensity. 'For all his drive,
for all his passion, Captain Jack was different from me
because he was happy. He was a happy person. And I
wanted to be happy too.'

She took a deep breath, gripping Jack's hands a bit too
tightly, judging from the grimace of pain that flashed
across his face.

'So, I told my camera people to stop rolling. I sent my
supermodel boyfriend — the father of my baby because
of his superior genes — I sent him a text saying that
it was over, that my life was on the sea now, and I let
Captain Jack take me. And I haven't stopped smiling
since.'

Captain Jack was crying now, great fat droplets of
seawater rolling down his face.

'That was beautiful, baby! Ah geez, what a lucky man I am. What did I ever do to deserve the love of a beautiful woman like this, and a wedding full of kidnapped teens on a boat? I ask ya, what did I do?' He reached out a beringed hand and stroked Gwynifred's face, moving aside the veil made of mosquito net.

'When I first saw Gwynifred Buren-Lee, I thought 'Who is this scary witch? Why does she have so many doilies? Why is she pickling everything she sees? Oh my god, what is she going to do to me?' And I tell you, that excited me in a way that a woman hasn't excited me in decades. Now, I've had a lot of wives. I've had Danish royalty, I've had freedom fighters, I've had jeep drivers and hang-gliders, I've had stern judges and sexy cabana boys. I've had it all. But you know what I've never had? I've never had a Gwynifred Buren-Lee, and I never in a thousand years thought I'd be lucky enough to find one.'

Jack paused, a thoughtful expression crossing his moustache.

'You know kids, there's a lot said about love. About where to find it, how to keep it and what it god darned is. And I can't say I have all the answers, I do not make that claim. But I do know that you can't go wrong if you never lose sight of how extraordinary the person you love is. So even when you hate each other, when you're throwing snakes at each other in a Las Vegas casino, screaming dire hexes — if you still think 'MY GOD THIS PERSON IS AMAZING' then there's a good chance you'll both come back from that. And even if you don't, your relationship will end on something beautiful, and that beautiful thing is respect. Not that I want my relationship with Gwynifred to end — but it's probably worth thinking about babe, because I'm probably going to be arrested by the government for kidnapping thirty at-risk teens.'

Kai brought the rings to them, and after urging her onwards, Izzy dolefully placed the plain metal bands onto the couple's fingers.

'Hot dog, Kai! These are great. Where did you get them from?'
'I just pulled the electric motor apart,' answered Kai proudly.
Captain Jack went green for a moment, but then clapped him on the shoulder. 'Hot dog indeed.'

'I now pronounce ourselves husband and wife, with the power invested in me by the ocean, by the undying ones who live in the trenches below, by the Great British navy and also secretly, the Spanish navy who sometimes hire me to be a pirate. I can now kiss the bride!'

Everyone cheered, and the Captain and Gwynifred kissed each other deeply and hungrily, Gwynifred's strong arms clawing at him for more.

'Uh folks,' announced Jack after he surfaced, 'me and the little lady have to go and do some marriage stuff now. I'm relying on you to sail this ship through the night! I'm also relying on you to keep playing this jazzy music for at least four more hours, you dig?'

With that, they disappeared into the captain's cabin, giggling and pawing at each other. Not long after that, the sound of their affection began to come through the walls, intermingling with Christina Aguilera and a song about the Venga bus. At first it sounded pretty standard, just groaning and moaning and giggling, but then it took off — it became screaming, name calling, shrieking. Things broke and shattered. It sounded like they were throwing each other around like sacks of flour and they were burly farmers. It was confronting, like accidentally listening to an elephant die painfully. Nobody knew what to do, except sail, sail into the night while passion rang around them.

After the caterwauling and thumping finally died down and blessed silence arrived, the wind also gave up and the ship slowed down to a stop. At first discipline reigned and everyone milled around doing small jobs, waiting for the wind and momentum to come back. And then Captain Jack emerged from his cabin, looking at first satisfied and replete, but then he sniffed the air hard and long, licking his finger and thrusting it into the sky.

'Oh. Oh no,' he muttered. 'Not today of all days, Thor! Not when I am so close to my goal!'
'What's the matter, sir?' asked Kai, good naturedly, slapping Jack on the back. The Captain flinched away from the hand, hissing at Kai spitefully. 'You idiot! Don't you see? It's the doldrums, the dead air itself, the death of sailors, the great ocean ennui! We're stuck!

Stuck here forever!'
'Um — we could use the motors though, right?' added
Heather, crossing her arms and looking serious.
'We could, if they hadn't been ripped apart for scrap!'
screamed Jack.

Kai looked at Captain Jack, his face slowly morphing
back into the sarcastic reserve that he wore before.

'Sorry, I didn't know,' he said quietly.
Captain Jack looked at him furiously and then ripped
the ring off his finger and threw it into the ocean. 'All
my work ... for nothing. We're going to miss the whale
hunt. All for nothing.'
'Jack?' asked a broken voice. It was Gwynifred, and she
looked at Jack's now naked ring finger. 'Don't I mean
anything to you?'

Jack stared at her, his jaw working furiously, his suit
hanging limply around him like the sails of the ship, like
the disappointed glares of his loyal crew.

'Just ... just leave me alone,' he muttered, slamming the
door of his cabin. 'Call me if the wind comes back.'

The discipline, the confidence and camaraderie
that Jack had painstakingly built up over the past
week disappeared along with the wind, and as the
day limped along, things got ugly. Gwynifred sat
down in the dark bunks, crying ugly tears, screaming
about how she'd thrown it all away for nothing. Her
cameraman, sans camera, sat with her awkwardly,
patting her on the back. Every so often, she would send

one of her cronies out for ingredients, for curses and poison brews that she mixed with her tears.

Up on the deck Kai almost immediately set to organising a game of football, which swiftly became violent and feral. A nose was broken and blood spattered the boards becoming an all-out brawl. Heather was flinging nerds left and right, while Kai turned on Brent, demolishing him with powerful, rage-filled punches to his kidneys and ribs and eyes. I'd already sniffed out the change in the air, with instincts hard won from long ago, with the kind of senses that a small rodent uses to intuit birds of prey circling above it. I hid, first in my favourite barrel hideaway, and then when it became obvious I was still too exposed — that at any moment those barrels might be tossed overboard — I went below deck, locking myself in a small utility closet, surrounded by darkness and hammers and spools of wire. There was no urine smell but there was also no way that a janitor would wander by and tell me it was safe to leave.

The air grew hot and charged, but still the ship stayed motionless, drifting slowly, alone and basting in our collective fear and disappointment. A few of the kids decided that it was time to call it quits, that they could radio home for help, for rescue. The debate grew heated, with people who didn't know what to do now, on this becalmed boat, knowing that they didn't want to go home, that they didn't want to admit defeat. But more and more people, who used the disgusting bathrooms, who scrounged away at the rapidly diminishing food, whose skin itched in the humid

air, more of them began to give up. And so finally a
delegate was chosen, to knock on the cabin door and to
request the radio from Captain Jack.

He answered, looking wild and unkempt. For the first
time, he had a thick layer of stubble over his face and
down his neck, obscuring his moustache. He wore
Bermuda shorts and a t-shirt that read 'Kiss Me, I'm
Awful'.

'What?' he asked irritably, the butt of a menthol
cigarette hanging from his lips.

'Well,' began Brent, speaking through puffed lips and
around a black eye.

'My god, what happened to you? Is it pirates? Have we
been boarded? Did the government find us?'

'No,' answered Brent with none of his usual vicious
jollity. 'Listen, we want to use the radio to call for help.
We wanna get off this ship. As you said, there's no
point anymore.'

Jack was quiet, his lips wobbling.

'No,' he said softly.

'Look, you can't ... you can't stop us,' cautioned Brent.

'Oh. Is that the way it is?' asked Jack, his nostrils
flaring. 'You think you can go a round of fisticuffs with
old Jack? These babies have pounded better men than
you, I'll tell you that. I once punched on with a shark,
and let's just say I was the one who swam away.'

Jack's fists were up like an old timey pugilist, his eyes
wide. 'I could, I could punch the whole lot of you ...
ah what's the point. Take the radio. Take my heart. I
don't care. What did I even think I was accomplishing.
I can't stop the whale hunt with an old wooden boat,

no matter the gumption of the crew. It's just not fast
enough. Damn me. Damn them and damn my pride.
They told me I couldn't pilot their ship anymore, and I
swore that I'd be there, no matter what. I tried to beg
and borrow every fast ship I could think of, until finally
this opportunity came up, this job as the captain for
a self-confidence exercise on the sea and I thought
— this is it, this is how I'll show them. They'll see that
Captain Jack Manning can't be kept away, here I am
on the most ludicrous ship I can think of! But I knew I
couldn't actually do anything to help the whales. I'm a
fraud. A fraud.'

His mighty head lowered, his slick hair in dishevelled
spikes, Captain Jack stood to the side and let Brent
go into the cabin, to put a stop to it all. The thought of
going home made me so happy, the thought of being
safe again. But even with that at the forefront of my
mind, my heart broke for Captain Jack. Before Brent
could work out how to get the radio going, there was a
scream from the rigging, a single word that sent a flush
of energy through the maudlin ship.

'STORM!'

Everyone turned to see Izzy, whose usually impassive
face was lit up by a deep purple sky, pointing behind
us at the thick dark bruise and swirling vortex that
boiled up from the west, obscuring the sun. If there
was one thing that had been drilled into us by the long-
forgotten navy personnel, it was the fear of a storm by
those crewing an old-fashioned wooden ship with sails.
Even a small squall could rip the Aspire to shreds, and

we had been taught a thousand ways to minimise the danger, despite the relative scarcity and size of the storms we were likely to face crawling up and down the coast of Australia. And now here we were, out in the middle of the ocean, caught in a tsunami.

The first gust of wind eddied past us, and it tasted charged and electric, dispelling the soporific heat that had lingered around the ship all day. And after that first gust came the whistling gale, howling over our heads. And, while everyone stood still looking at each other and at Jack standing defeated and broken, one of Gwynifred's disciples raced onto the deck, ignoring the gathering storm, ignoring the face-off between the Captain and his crew.

'Help!' she cried.

Nobody answered.

'Help!' she tried again. 'It's Gwynifred! Her water just broke!'

BOATJACK

III

The storm roared all around the SS Youth Aspire. The air was full of the deep booms of thunder, the crackling of lightning that lit the tableau with actinic brightness, like flash photographs of wet, terrified people. The ship climbed huge waves, dumped into the troughs, tipping wildly, washing the decks with giant fists of cold saltwater, wiping away the remnants of the wedding from the night before, and threatening to wipe away the underage crew, who held onto ropes, who had donned their long-forgotten life vests. But above it all, over the sound of nature screaming and grumbling and cursing, was the sound of Gwynifred Buren-Lee giving birth. She roared and cursed and keened like a banshee, and there wasn't a single person on board the ship who had any idea of what to do.

'Ah geez Jacky boy, you've got yourself into a hell of a mess this time,' muttered Captain Jack, hanging on with one hand outside the bunks, below deck where he'd been banished after trying to help.

'Get out! You sack of crap, you dirty fucking disappointment hole, you heartbreaker, you ass dangle!' she'd cried, face red, body heaving.

'I just want to help out, babe. Let me make it up to you,' he pleaded.

'I will drown you in my placenta. I will give birth to a sword just to cut your toes off. Get out, get out!'

'But honeybits ...'

'I will give birth to a pig with your face which will follow you for the rest of your life if you don't move.'

Now he stood outside the room wringing his hands and covering his ears to the guttural screams ripping through the bulkhead. One of Gwynifred's disciples came running out, slamming the door behind her.

'I never want to see again!' she cried.

'Oh geez,' whined Captain Jack.

Up above, there was a loud, meaty crack as one of the smaller sections of mast was bent to the extreme by the tsunami, snapping off and crashing onto the deck, smashing the barrels that both Izzy and I habitually hid behind. For me, terrified and cold and wet, it was only an escalation of a bad situation. For Izzy, it was the moment when, like the mast, she snapped. She grabbed me, and without words steered me to the pumping mechanism, which we'd been trained together to use. She pointed stiffly, her face angry

and motivated, like a business bull. I started it up —
having a ship that wasn't full of water was a great idea.
Izzy stormed over to Kai, grabbing him by his sodden
t-shirt. For the first time, I noticed she was taller than
him, that once her body was uncurled from whatever
sullen position she was in, she was long and powerful,
like a python.

'You — whatever your name is. Shitface! Get your little
boyfriends to start tightening the mainsail.'
Kai struggled against her, his face sour.
'Fuck you, freak!'
'Real original you crap hole but I'm not dying on this
goddamn boat so we need to start doing something
with this storm. We need to do all this crap that we
were trained to do.'

Anyone who wasn't trying to help with the live
childbirth happening below deck gathered around
Izzy. There was something about her voice — so barely
used, now surprisingly strident and loud and clear —
that grabbed everyone's attention over the sound of
the storm and pain and wind and thunder. Water was
pouring down the hatches, so grabbing hold of the
ropes on the deck was just as safe as anywhere else.

'Listen. You've all fucked up. You all let yourself get
talked into Captain Jack's ridiculous dreams of
saving whales and being all you can be. We're all here
because we're fuckups, and he told us that we can be
something other than fuckups. Sailors or whale heroes
or whatever. And that all worked for you but now he's
disappointed you and you all feel sad or whatever. Well,

boo-hoo! Poor you! People are shit, get over it. People are going to try and tell you what to think your entire life. Here's a little lesson: listen to none of them.'

Izzy paused for a breath, water dripping down her impassioned face.

'This is really motivational,' muttered Kai.
'Shut the fuck up, you fuckhole,' Izzy spat. 'What I'm saying is that by letting yourself get all sad and butthurt because your weird boat messiah ended up being a crapstick is bullshit. He did nothing. You're the ones who sailed this ship all this way, and you're the ones who are gonna get off your asses and make sure this ship doesn't sink. And you can sail wherever you goddamn want. You can sail back home, you can ride this crazy storm into an active fleet of whalers and save a whale, you can sail it into your dad's dickhole, I don't care but you are going to goddamn sail this fucking ship.'

There was an appalled silence, or at least as much of a silence as there could be when the sky was throwing lightning bolts and bitter-cold water and a woman was screaming a person out of her uterus. And then Kai, with the storm's eye passing overhead and a grin plastered across his stupid beautiful face, said 'Aye, aye, Captain.'

Everyone broke away. Lines were hauled, the ship was straightened out, its sails taut with strain and pressure as it rode the gale to the east. Instead of lumbering over waves and falling down the depressions, it sliced

through them, like a knife, like a shark. Izzy stood
at the captain's wheel, arms straining to push the
wheel against the entire ocean, her face serious and
deadly and beautiful. And behind her came a slow
clapping.

Clap. Clap. Clap.

It was Captain Jack, and he was smiling at her.

'So, the student becomes the master.'
'Go die in a ditch,' said Izzy, not even looking behind.
'I always knew you had it in you, that behind that
façade lay the heart of a sea captain. I knew that if I just
let you be yourself, the true Izzy would come forth, like
one of those tiny rolled towels that you add water to.
And I knew that if I stepped back, let the ship run itself,
you would finally stand up and take your rightful place.
And look at you, you're magnificent.'
'Are you honestly telling me that you did this on
purpose? That you had a weird crisis of faith and
offended your new wife just so I'd … take your place?
Even if I half believed that, it's unsound logic! Actually,
maybe I do believe that.'

Captain Jack spread his hands wide. 'Listen, snacky-
cakes, it might not have been the ideal situation for
it to happen, but I always planned on letting you take
the reins at some point. The truth is that I speak big,
but I'm a realist. Even if we do somehow manage to get
to the whale hunt in time, it will only be a statement, a
gesture, a symbol. And those are important, don't get
me wrong. A symbol of defiance from Captain Jack.

But we won't save any whales.'

Izzy looked at him curiously, a calculating look on her face, like a snake deciding which bird egg to eat.

'You'll see you goddamn puke, you ocean lecher, you crap hole'.

Captain Jack stared back and then started doing a little jig.

'Hot damn, hot dog. Are you saying we're going to sail into the whaling fields? We're gonna hit the whale hunt?'

Izzy shrugged, the storm blowing her hair all around her face.

'If we don't die first, then yeah — seems like all these assholes want to keep sailing. And the way I see it we have to sail somewhere, so we might as well go and stop a bunch of whales from dying. Whales are great. They're like big ocean dogs.'
'Gee whiz, you sound like me, Izzy!' chortled Captain Jack.
'Yeah, except I mean it. We're going to save some whales.'

The thing about Izzy is that on this boat, she was truly the strangest kid there. A lot of us had been given a raw deal because of how we were born: systemic racism, the patriarchy, homophobia, transphobia, ableism, a witch's curse. Some of us had bad parents,

they were drug addicts, alcoholics or just plain
neglectful. There's a whole gamete of bad shit that
happened to the currently mutinying crew of the SS
Youth Aspire. But none of them had been born into
Izzy St. James' family. I only know this story now, in
retrospect, after the press pored over our lives, and
the newspapers ran stories about Izzy's life from
interviews with her bewildered, clueless parents.

The SS Youth Aspire sailed on the crest of the storm
like a kite, pushed at astronomical speed by the
tsunami-class winds. The ship cracked and groaned
under the stress, everything taut and tight and
humming with pain. Bits of the ship snapped off, shed
like a really fast snake who was impatiently emerging
from its skin as an even leaner, quicker snake. Over
the course of the night, while the storm spent its fury,
they sailed two days' worth of distance, their efforts to
capture the might of the wind in their sails successful.
And Izzy stood behind it all, screaming orders over
the wind, cursing and yelling and laughing, while
everyone pulled their weight, past exhaustion, past
comprehension.

Captain Jack would later tell anyone who would stop
and listen for long enough that it was the best sailing
he'd ever seen, that it was like watching tiny gods
work magic, that they taught him a thing or two. He
would take a sip of his drink, let it dribble down his
chin and proclaim, 'They're my children in every way
that counts. I built them with my own two hands,
crafted them out of lies and promises, played their
egos and their raw senses of isolation and hurt with

my masterful words. Oh yes, they're my babies. Much more so than Tina and Henri, my actual biological children who are a giant disappointment. Maybe it was hard growing up in the shadow of a boat full of teens, maybe that's the problem.'

When the sun rose the storm finally spent its fury and disappeared with a whimper, leaving the sky washed and blue, the sea green and calm and the SS Youth Aspire battered, but not broken. And now that the wind had stopped yelling, something else could be heard: the squalling of a newborn child.

'I will name her Aspire,' croaked Gwynifred, cradling the child, which looked like a sneezed out clot of blood and gunge. Gwynifred was a mess; she really needed a hospital, because childbirth is difficult. But the intensity in which she'd trained her pelvic floor before the birth had paid off, and she wasn't bleeding out, which is good news because honestly they should have been sailing towards a medical professional, instead of into a fleet of bloodthirsty whalers.

'Now kids, there's gonna be a whole bunch of huge modern ships, with harpoons and guns and motors that could pulverise us, and the important thing is to not be scared. They will get in a lot of trouble if they kill us, so they will have to be careful around us. Probably what we'll do is sail around, and distract them, because they've probably never seen such an old wooden boat before. Yeah — distraction is the name of the game, and they're less likely to kill us.'

We were less than an hour away from the place where the whale hunt began. Jack was amped but nervous. He was in business mode, ready to conduct his long-awaited campaign.

'We had these great concussion grenade things that we used on the Ocean Guardian. Any science nerds on this boat who could knock one up? That would be helpful.'

But as we sailed into range, Jack frowned. 'There's way too many boats. Have the bastards expanded? Are they amping up things? Is this their final push to invade the whales' undersea homes?'

Soon we could see it all — there were six big whaling ships clustered together on the horizon. No whale carcasses hung from the sides like trophies and no harpoons were being shot in the water. There were not even any crew visible. They huddled inside, windows darkened, hiding from the eyes of the world's media. Because around the whaling ships were news helicopters from all over the world, from Australia, from the BBC, from CNN, Al Jazeera, everywhere. And in the water, speeding towards the Youth Aspire, were Australian navy boats, the coast guard and choppy little police boats, with their blue and white sirens flashing.

'By Thor's angry wang,' exclaimed Captain Jack in wonderment and confusion. 'How on earth did this happen? What the buggery is going on?'

As they watched, the whalers started up their

huge motors and turned around. There was simply too much media scrutiny for them to risk their whaling endeavours. It was known that they would 'accidentally' spear more whales than their 'scientific charter' allowed them to, especially going for mothers with baby whales, and bigger, rarer whales. In an official statement made later that day, the whalers stated that the hunt for that year had been called off, due to fears of accidentally hurting any of the media or other boats that swarmed the area. But really it was because we had won. It was because of Izzy.

'How did you DO this?' screamed Captain Jack on his knees in front of Izzy, who couldn't stop herself from grinning with triumph and pleasure.

'Whatever,' she said, walking away from the Captain, who looked like he was suffering a religious ecstasy, who stayed down on his knees, arms raised towards the sky. He knew the whale hunt was over, that somehow, after years of striving, he had been successful, at least for one year.

As for Izzy's ways, I later saw the video she'd recorded, once I was back on the mainland, eating biscuits with my grandmother. It turns out that while the rest of us were being transformed and brainwashed and mutineering with Captain Jack, Izzy had been striking up a very tentative, very surprising friendship with the most invisible person on the ship: Gwynifred Buren-Lee's cameraman, a twenty-four-year-old named Bradley Law. Bradley had watched first as a mutiny happened around him, and then as his erstwhile employer (Gwynifred Buren-Lee) had gone mad and shacked up with the pirate captain. He'd been told by a mildly threatening Captain Jack that his job was no longer relevant and he had to stop filming. Scared, alone and confused, Bradley tried to hide as all the weirdness unraveled: the mutinies, the becalming, the wedding, the birth, the storm. And while he hid, he met Izzy. And Bradley was such a quiet, gentle lumberjack puppy of a man, all kind eyes and soft beard and helpless hands, that Izzy took pity on him, and stopped swearing at him and spitting whenever she saw him. And for lack of anything better to do, he told her about his job, about filming *Doing IT Right*, and about how his camera and live feed worked. And when Izzy decided to save the whales, she recorded this message.

'Hello, my name is Izzy St. James and I was raised as a dog. But that isn't important right now — the important thing is that I'm one of thirty kids who have stolen an old wooden ship.'

The picture is a little grainy, due to the bad quality of light; she's filming in the supply closet during the storm. You can hear wind and thunder in the background, and occasionally the cry of a TV star giving birth.

'I don't know if people know that we're missing yet. I assume so because we are days overdue. Well, here we are. You can find us at this location.'

The coordinates of where the whale hunt was to start flashed up on the screen.

'You should probably come and find us. We are a bunch
of missing teens after all. Oh, and Gwynifred Buren-
Lee is with us, and she's literally giving birth right
now. That's pretty important. Oh, and she's shacked
up with the captain of this ship. You shouldn't blame
the captain either — it's all of us kids who mutinied
— we just decided to keep him around to help us sail
the ship. He was very against this whole thing. You
shouldn't arrest him. OH! And you should really try
to rescue all the navy sailors that we put in a life raft. I
hope they're OK.'

Izzy's stern, unhappy face paused for a while, glitched
a bit and then refocused.

'I have to go and sail this ship now. But you should send
the media. There's a lot of underage sex going on. Bye!'

The media went nuts for the story and every kid on
board the ship became a minor celebrity when they got
back.

Captain Jack made one appearance on a talk show,
wearing a zebra-striped zoot suit, looking sharp and
greasy and charming as hell. He looked like the very
devil himself.

'Why do you think the kids stole the SS Youth Aspire?'
asked the smiling blonde host.
'Why? Why? Because I'm proud as hell of them.'
The host blinked and continued gamely.
'Do you think this is indicative of their generation
— a kind of selfishness, an inability to understand

consequences?'

'I think it's indicative of the best kind of cats; the kinds of people who don't just meekly accept whatever shit has been served before them, who look up from their poo salad and say, 'hell no. I shall have something else!' Baby, these kids had the strength of mind to make a big difficult decision, to literally sail against the tide of expectation and popular opinion and birth circumstances. And against all odds, they managed to change the world for the better. Maybe only for one season, but that's more than most people can claim. These funky cats are gonna end up doing wonderful things. Maybe they'll run this country from the parliament, maybe they'll run against it, maybe they'll be bold enough to live in the desert, eating lizards and making tin hats so that Facebook can't find them. Whatever it is, I know they'll have the strength of mind to do it with passion and conviction and certainty. All because of a boat. A big old wooden ship, which they sailed into international waters. Now baby, I've prepared a little song for the situation.'

Captain Jack stood up, pulling out a saxophone from behind the couch, and he played, played until they went to an ad break.

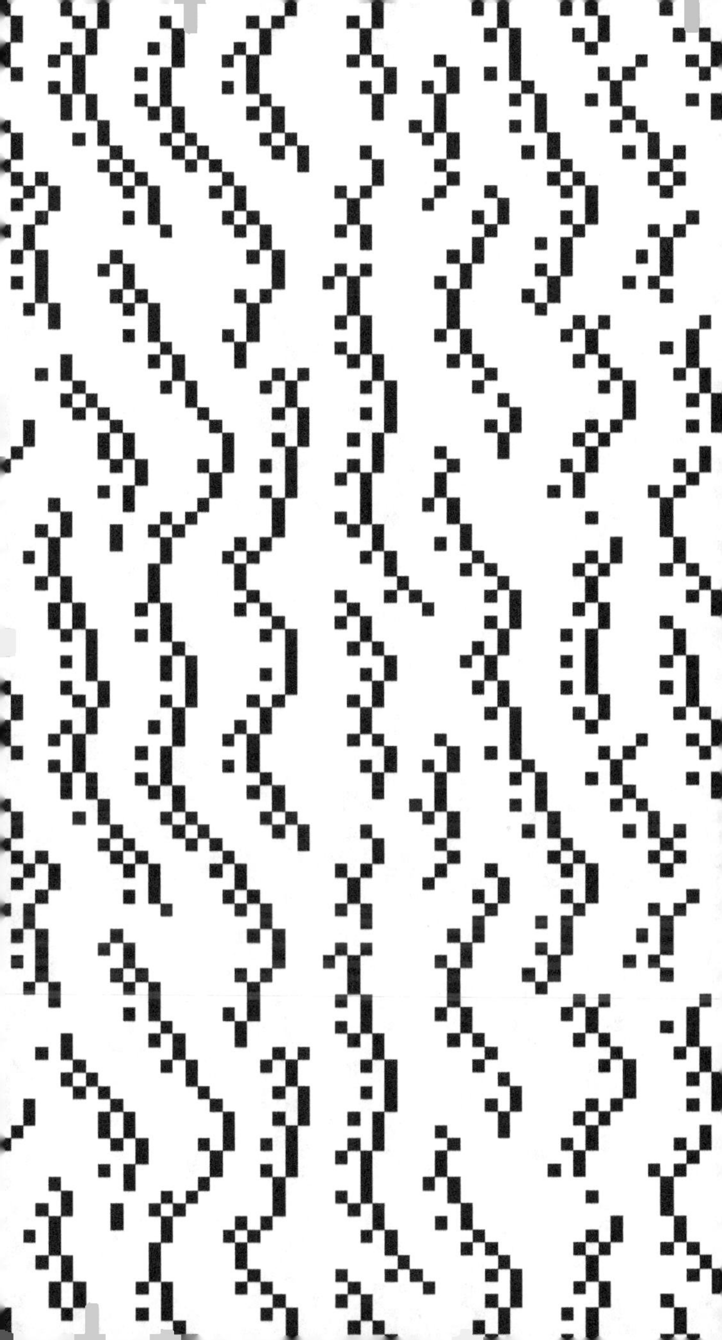

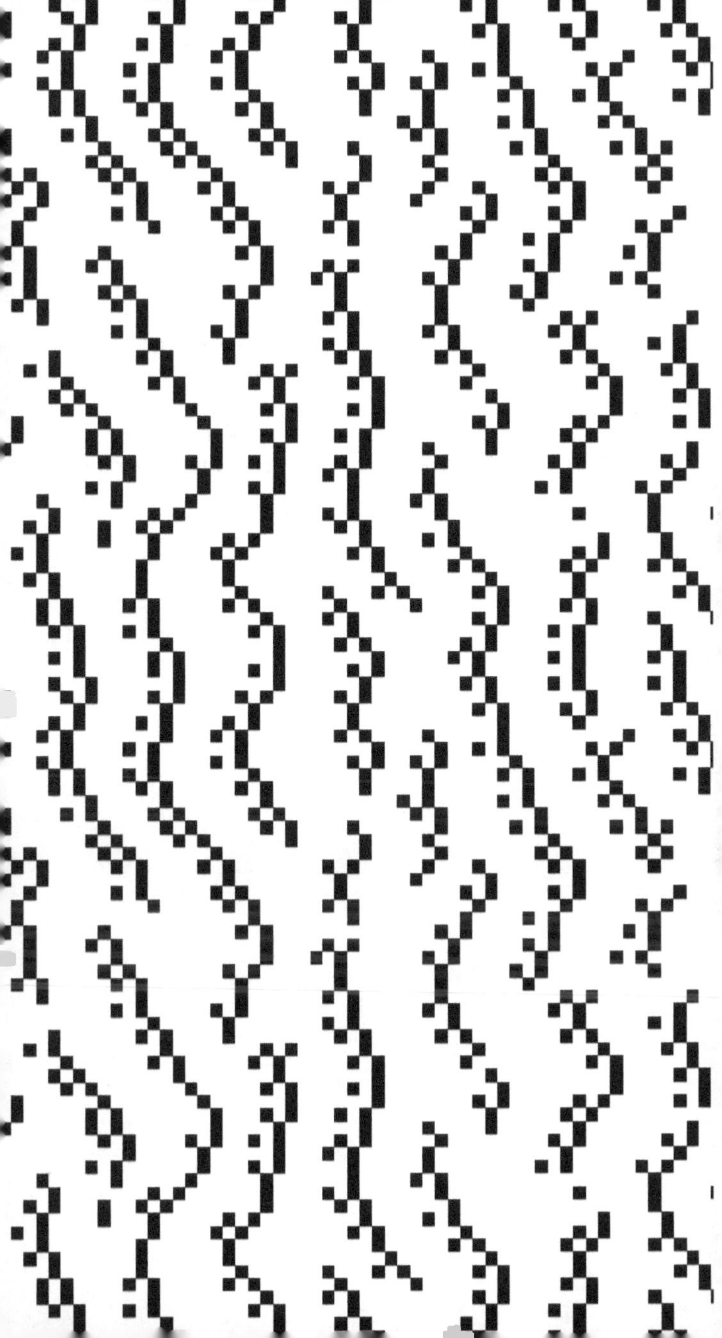

ACKNOWLEDGEMENTS

'Home is where the dad is' previously appeared in
Better Read Than Dead Writing Anthology 2020

'Dog Park' previously appeared in *Scum Magazine*

'Homing Pigeon' was the winner of the Aniko Press
Summer Flash Fiction Competition 2021

A version of 'Boatjack' was shortlisted for the Seizure
Viva La Novella Prize and the Griffith Novella Competition

ACKNOWLEDGEMENTS

A huge thank you to angel and light of my life
Samira Lloyd, who was the first person to read this
manuscript. Her completely spontaneous delivery of
notes, thoughts, and enthusiasm was such a brilliant
gift, and a very specific type of love-language between
friends who are stupid enough to have studied creative
writing together. Thank you to the best person in the
world, Emma Wortley, for workshopping *43 rats* and
being great.

I'd like to thank Rick Morton, Julie Koh, and Nina
Oyama for blurbing this book, such a lovely thing to do
for someone.

I'd also like to thank the original inspiration for the
title of this book, the Sexy Tales Comedy Collective.
For much of my twenties, a rag-tag band of the most
delightful weirdos I know believed in me and my
writing so much that they were willing to tour and
perform three of my plays around Australia. Everyone
involved is a very treasured part of my life, and the title
of this book is partly a homage to the stupid art we
made and our time together.

And finally I want to thank Dan Hogan and Victoria
Manifold from Subbed In. I get to see a glimpse of
how hard they work on this project, somehow juggling
day jobs and their own writing. Subbed In is so
special and perfect and rare in the hellfire that is the
Australian publishing industry, and their work is wildly
appreciated by me and lovers of weird writing. Thank
you for believing in this very stupid book!

ABOUT THE AUTHOR

Patrick Lenton is an author and journalist from Melbourne. He is the author of *A Man Made Entirely of Bats* (Spineless Wonders), collection of essays *Uncle Hercules and Other Lies* (Subbed In), and full-length collection of short stories *Sexy Tales of Paleontology* (Subbed In). His writing has been featured in *The Best Australian Stories*, *The Best Australian Comedy Writing*, *Growing Up Queer In Australia*, and journals like *Kill Your Darlings*, *Going Down Swinging*, *Scum Magazine*, and more. He is the Editor of pop-culture, news, and entertainment website *Junkee* and has written journalism and non-fiction for publications including *The Guardian*, *Sydney Morning Herald*, *VICE*, and more.

ABOUT SUBBED IN

Subbed In is an independent literararararararararary organisation and (very) small publisher. Subbed In programs events and publishes award-winning books that aim to elevate the voices of First Nations people, trans people, people of colour, non-binary people, sex workers, women, people with a disability, LGBTQIA+ people, survivors, working class people, and anyone who finds themselves on the margins of the supremely white, cis, heteronormative, capitalist, colonial, ableist, patriarchal hellscape in which we live. We jam econo.

www.subbed.in

ALSO AVAILABLE FROM SUBBED IN

apocalypse scroll like it was normal
by kenji kinz

In The Drink
by Emily Crocker

*When I die slingshot my ashes
onto the surface of the moon*
by Jennifer Nguyen

blur by the
by Cham Zhi Yi

HAUNT (THE KOOLIE)
by Jason Gray

The Hostage
by Šime Knežević

*If you're sexy and you know
it slap your hams*
by Eloise Grills

wheeze
by Marcus Whale

Parenthetical Bodies
by Alex Gallagher

The Naming
by Aisyah Shah Idil

Girls and Buoyant
by Emily Crocker

Uncle Hercules and other lies
by Patrick Lenton

www.subbed.in

Girls and
Buoyant
Emily Crocker

blur
by
the
Cham Zhi Yi

THE
HOSTAGE

wh
ee
ze

If you're sexy
and you know it
slap your hams

Uncle Hercules
and other lies
Patrick Lenton

HAUNT
(THE KOOLIE)
JASON GRAY

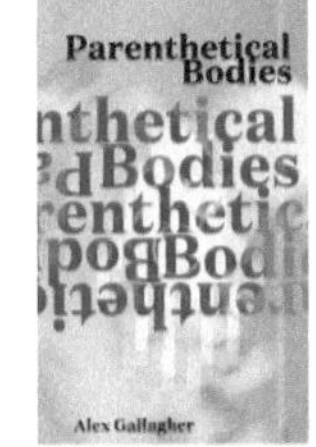

Parenthetical
Bodies
Alex Gallagher

The
Naming
Alayah Shah Idil

sexy tales
of paleontology
patrick lenton

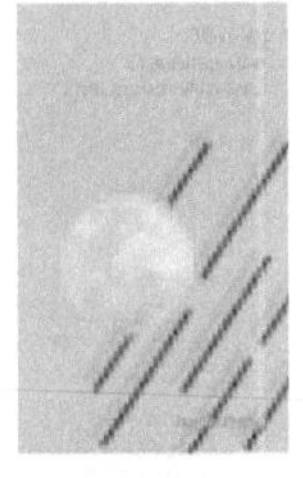

IN THE
DRINK
EMILY CROCKER

www.ingramcontent.com/pod-product-compliance
Lightning Source LLC
Chambersburg PA
CBHW020123120726
47903CB00007B/2074